The Blackmailer

A BLACK BAT MYSTERY

By the same author
THE NIGHT HUNTERS
THE SILVER BULLET GANG

The Blackmailer

BY JOHN MILES

THE BOBBS-MERRILL COMPANY, INC.
INDIANAPOLIS   NEW YORK

Copyright © 1974 by John Miles
All rights reserved, including the right of reproduction
in whole or in part in any form
Published by the Bobbs-Merrill Company, Inc.
Indianapolis   New York

ISBN 0-672-51934-8
Library of Congress catalog card number 73-22660
Designed by Jack Jaget
Manufactured in the United States of America
First printing

One

DENSE August humidity made the Washington skyline purple-blue. In the traffic-clogged streets below the hotel window, cars crept along in the hazy glare of their own exhaust fumes. Night was coming on.

Walking with an almost angry briskness to the hotel window, Joe Graeber jerked the drapery cords, shooting the pale curtains fully closed to blot out the scene. He was a big man, going to fat, balding. What was left of his hair was combed from ear to ear and slicked down to hide his baldness. His black suit was a little old-fashioned, with narrow, rounded lapels, and pleats that gave the trousers too much fullness at the top, tapering to cuffs cut too tightly. His shoes were black and thick-soled, cumbersome in a way that recalled the Eisenhower years. Graeber looked like a man clinging to 1950.

He had already subjected the hotel room to a methodical, painstaking search while the other two men sat on the couch, waiting. Now, with the draperies closed, he took a small electronic gadget from his coat pocket, flicked it on, and stared at a needle on the face. The instrument was about the size of a pocket computer, but it obviously had another use.

The two men on the couch, wearing nondescript business suits, watched him silently. They were a little younger, in their thirties. One, Collins, was sandy-haired and husky. The other, Schmidt, betrayed a slight testiness that fit his lean, nervous build.

Graeber continued to frown at his instrument, walking around the room and pointing the device this way and that as he twiddled a dial.

Schmidt finally spoke explosively, as if unable to restrain himself. "It isn't bugged, Joe. It can't be bugged. We just walked in, and nobody knows we're in the city."

Graeber's face wrinkled, beefy and intent, but showed no other sign of having heard. He walked around the room with the detector, disappeared into the bathroom for a moment, returned, and finally switched the instrument off and put it back into his coat pocket. He went over and turned on the TV set, paying no attention to channel selection. An early evening quiz show appeared on the screen. He turned up the volume so the sound filled the room, then walked over to the chair facing the couch, hiked up his trousers and sat down.

"You have the pictures?" he asked.

Collins opened an attaché case, removed an eleven-by-fourteen brown envelope, and handed it over. Graeber took the envelope, did not open it, but put it on the edge of the coffee table. "Good. Might not need them. But they ought to maximize my appeal, if that's needed."

The TV set blared with audience applause. Schmidt twitched. "Can't we turn that down a little?"

"No. You know better."

"No one could possibly know we're here, Joe!"

Graeber glowered from under heavy eyelids. "It's procedure."

Schmidt took a long, slow breath but said nothing.

Graeber turned to Collins again. "I'll make contact tomorrow at fourteen hundred hours or Thursday at the same time. If those two contacts fail, I'll call in the clear Friday night at your home. If I call Friday night, I'll give you a number, inverted, where you can contact me from a secure telephone one hour after my call to you. Understood?"

Collins nodded, his face showing nothing.

"Whatever happens, I want you on that flight to Cincinnati next Tuesday. You understand how you're to proceed?"

"I rent a car, drive to Columbus, turn that car in and buy something used but dependable, with cash. I change the plates and go to the cabin."

Graeber turned to Schmidt.

"I go Monday," Schmidt said wearily.

"How?"

"Air. Pittsburgh, Cleveland, Chicago, Indianapolis, Dayton."

"And bus to Columbus," Graeber prodded.

"And bus to Columbus. Right."

"And I pick you up."

"Yes."

"You have the equipment?"

"The guns? . . . Yes."

Graeber nodded. "I have someone who can probably do this with us. But I want Jane." He tapped the brown envelope. "With these I can get her. She might not like it, but I can get her."

Schmidt asked, "How about the other people?"

"You'll meet them next week."

"Who are they?"

Graeber's eyes hooded. "You don't need that information now."

"Don't you think we ought to know who we'll be working with?"

"They don't know you and you don't know them. That's SOP."

"There *isn't* any standard operating procedure, Joe. This isn't CIA anymore!"

"It worked then. It works now. It always works. This is just as tricky as anything any of us ever did for the agency or anybody else."

"You think I don't know that? Going onto that floor of the lodge, with all those people around? When I think what might happen—"

"Nothing will happen," Graeber said stolidly. "We follow SOP and it's all routine."

"The guns don't make it routine."

"Only an extreme emergency would require using them or anything else."

Schmidt's head jerked. "What's 'anything else'?"

"We'll have an explosive device."

"You didn't say anything about that."

"It's only for the most extreme emergency. It could be detonated as a diversionary tactic."

"On the floor?"

"On the floor. But I won't even consider using it except as a last resort."

Schmidt looked a little pale. He swallowed and said nothing.

Collins said, "I figure, if Jane is stubborn despite everything, you can still get the other person."

"Yes," Graeber said. "No doubt about that."

The three men sat in the din of the TV set; someone on the show had just won a Vega.

"Questions?" Graeber asked.

"The money," Collins said.

Graeber produced a fat billfold and peeled off hundred-dollar bills, thirty of them. Then he counted off a dozen more, dividing them into equal stacks. "Car money. Expense money. You both have the earlier allowance."

Schmidt and Collins pocketed the cash.

Graeber stood. "That does it, then." He paused a moment as if trying to think of anything he might have overlooked. Then he turned and walked to the door, opened it, and left the room.

Humming tunelessly, Collins went over and shut off the TV set. He gave Schmidt a ruefully amused glance. "Breath of fresh air?"

The draperies were opened and the two men stepped out onto the tiny balcony, into the heat of the Washington night. The traffic below was just as bad as before, and now the sun had fully set. The heat pressed in. Schmidt and Collins stood on the balcony in silence for a little while, Schmidt fidgeting, Collins milky-eyed and stoical.

"He's crazy," Schmidt said finally.

Collins grinned.

"The son of a bitch is really crazy," Schmidt said.

"It's a big thing for him. He almost had it a couple of months ago, you know, and somebody blew it at the plant. That one guy will probably end up in the state pen on account of it. This is probably the last chance."

"I know the engine is important," Schmidt said patiently. "I know it means a lot of money to a lot of people. I know the risks and I know we'll probably get a lot more work through Joe if it goes well. But the way he's going at it is insane; that's all there is to it."

"Let him play his little games. Hell."

"We have a nice job of industrial espionage to do," Schmidt snapped. "They have their security people, and we have our plans to get around the security people. Fine. We need a crew and we need careful planning. Fine. If we get caught, we're felons, and we go to prison, so we damned sure don't want to get caught. *Fine*. . . . But some of this code stuff, and staggered departures, and his paranoia about bugging, are just ridiculous."

"As long as his craziness takes the form of extra precautions, we should resent it? His precautions might save our asses."

"It's the way he goes at it all! My God, he still thinks we're planning the Bay of Pigs invasion or something!"

Collins was silent a moment, then shrugged. "Maybe that was the high point of his life."

"The Bay of Pigs?"

"He was high up, wasn't he? He had power, money, an elaborate clandestine operation, people who were fanatically loyal. Then it turned to worms. What the hell did he ever get out of it? It wasn't his fault the invasion failed. He did his part right. But instead of being credited for it, he was one of those shunted out, written off the books as if he never existed. Ever since then he's been scrambling. When that Sandresko operation failed a few years ago, anybody else would have been either caught or ruined by it. Not Joe Graeber. Goddamn, here he comes right back, still scrambling. I heard he even had White House connections for a while, before Watergate. Now he's down again, but this is another chance. Maybe his biggest yet. Why shouldn't he be extra careful? Why shouldn't he act like it was still the sixties? The sixties were the high point of his life."

"I just don't like it," Schmidt grunted.

"You didn't have to accept."

"You know what I've been doing? I've been a security officer at a high school. At a *high school*."

"Then don't bitch."

"I'm not bitching. All I'm saying—"

9

"Look," Collins cut in, "this worries me too. If it didn't, I'd be crazy too. But as many security agencies as this country has operated in the last twenty years—and as many purges as we've seen—ex-agents are about as much in demand as old-lady poets. This country is crawling with trained security operatives begging for work. I went to a college reunion last winter and recognized seven guys there who were—or had been—agents. Seven! It was a small college. We're damned lucky to have a job where we can do what we do best."

Schmidt nervously lighted a cigarette. "Look at his preoccupation with this chick we used in the Sandresko deal. She isn't all that well trained."

"She's a beautiful woman."

"She's also married now, and out of it. Do you think Joe wants her because she's the only one who could do that part? Hell, no. He wants her because he's living in the past."

Collins hummed as if amused. "He'll get her, too."

"And did you hear what he said about an explosive device, for Christ's sake? He's going in there with an S-16 type of bomb, probably, and he says he'll use it only in an extreme emergency. He'll detonate the thing, and take out a whole floor of a hotel, with forty or fifty people on that floor, only in 'an emergency.' Jesus!"

"Do you want out?" Collins asked.

"No, I don't want out. I'm just worried, that's all."

"Well, then, relax. Joe Graeber played the game a long time by a given set of rules and assumptions. A leopard can't change its spots. There isn't any right or wrong for you when you've played the game as long as Graeber has. There are just results. There are just jobs and systems and results, and everything else—laws, or right and wrong, or anything else—is just shadows."

Schmidt looked down at the city, and his lean face worked as he tried to sort things out in his own mind. He looked like a caged animal.

Finally he said, "I'm in it all the way. Don't get me wrong. I'm committed. But going after that girl, taking explosives, using guns, all his code names and anti-bugging devices—those are all crazy things. I don't mind doing a lot of things, but I'm not wild about working on a job where killing people is accepted as a routine option. Not on a job where we're totally outside and nobody is standing behind us . . . nobody at all."

"Trust Joe," Collins suggested. "That's all you can do."

"Right," Schmidt said heavily. "That's precisely what bothers me. Because he doesn't know what year it is. He's nuts. He'd do *anything*. We're working for Joe Graeber, and he's crazy as a hoot owl."

"Well," Collins said, "it takes all kinds."

Two

MILO RUSH walked up the tree-lined fairway and found his ball about eighty yards from the green. The eighteenth green was small and well trapped, with water in front and the Victorian bulk of the clubhouse not far behind it. The pin was on the front edge only a dozen paces from the edge of the water, and, despite the hazy afternoon heat, there were several club members on the patio nearby, probably enjoying the hilarity of shots hit boldly for the flag; a few feet short, and it was hello lily pads.

Rush waited while two of his playing partners babied up to the water and the third hit into the back trap. Using his wedge, he lofted the ball high against the muggy sky and watched it drop hole-high and about ten feet to the right of the pin.

"Way to hit, partner!"

Crossing the bridge to reach the green, Rush noticed the man standing behind the green. Rush held up his hand, and Dave Clarken, looking hot and uncomfortable in his dark business suit, waved back.

Rush walked around the green. "Hello, David. What's going on?"

Clarken smiled thinly. "Nice shot."

Noting Clarken's pallor, Rush did not bother to acknowledge the compliment. "What is it, Dave?"

"I need to talk."

Turning, Rush gestured to his caddy. "Pick it up. I'll see you in the pro shop later." He turned back to go with Clarken.

"No," Clarken said. "Putt out. Finish. Christ."

They had been friends a long time, and Rush had never seen Clarken like this. Something serious had happened. But Clarken's twisted face showed he really wanted to see the game finished first, as if normalcy were desperately important and not just a matter of politeness. Rush shrugged and awaited his turn to play.

The two members of the foursome who had hit short of the water, then come across, needed long putts to salvage their pars. Both missed. Rush's playing partner came out of the back trap weakly and then putted well past. Rush grinned with their banter, but he was observing Clarken out of the corner of his eye. When he lined up his own birdie try, he was preoccupied and hit it badly. He took the par tap-in, made his apologies for skipping the drinks in the locker room, and rejoined his friend.

"Can you use a drink, Dave?"

Clarken, who was almost as tall as Rush, was so pale his freckles stood out sharply. "Maybe I could use one."

"The bar is a good place to talk. Come on."

Saying nothing, Clarken followed him around the side of the enormous clubhouse, past the patio area, and to the entrance customarily used by members wearing spiked shoes. The cool of air conditioning wrapped itself around Rush's body as he went inside. He led Clarken down a carpeted hallway and into the large bar area with its high paneled walls and dark-beamed ceiling. After the hazy glare of afternoon, it seemed very dark. Two men were drinking at the bar and a couple sat at one table. Rush led the way to a table on the far side, well away from everyone.

Clarken sat down and glanced around warily, with the air of a man trying very hard to look at home. "It's a hell of a place, Milo."

Give him time, Rush thought. "The course is great. You're about due to come out and play with me again, aren't you?"

"I haven't been playing."

"You need to. You look a little strung out."

Clarken took a deep breath. He looked more than a little strung out. There was a caged look in his eyes, and his hands trembled as he lighted a cigarette. He seemed about to speak, but the waitress came over and took their order for the drinks.

He was, Rush knew, thirty-five years old, an investments counselor in one of the big Washington firms. Rush had met him ten years earlier, immediately after winning the Consolidated Fabrics case, when there was a very nice fee to invest and Clarken was with Merrill Lynch. The routine business contact had started a friendship which, while not fed by constant contact, had remained warm. Rush had not seen him for three months now and was shocked by his appearance.

Clarken seemed unable to get to the point. "Maybe I ought to join one of these clubs . . . get out more."

"You could have a membership here."

"Too rich for my blood."

"It's not really that high."

"I mean I don't know how I'd fit in."

"You'd fit in fine."

"There are some awfully wealthy people around here."

"The nice thing about the very rich, Dave, is that they tend to polarize. The ones who have decent tendencies seem to become more decent, and finer, because the pressure is off."

Clarken's lips twitched. "And the others?"

Rush shrugged. "They become grotesque. And to hell with them."

The girl brought the drinks. Clarken had ordered a martini on the rocks, and now he clutched the fat glass with both hands as if it were a lifeline. "Business has been good," he said, staring off into a vacant corner like a driven man.

"Good," Rush said.

"Trading is sluggish, of course, but it's an interesting time."

Rush said nothing.

"Jane is fine," Clarken added.

"I'm glad to hear it."

Clarken put down his glass and leaned forward. "Milo, I don't know what in the hell to *do*."

"What's happened?"

"It's Jane. Jesus Christ, Milo. I think I'm—I think something is going on, and I don't know what it is or how to deal with it!"

Rush hesitated. The suffering in Clarken's eyes was so intense it hurt him. He knew he should not be surprised that Jane might be involved. As an attorney, he met all sorts of ugly marriage breakups all too often, even though now he accepted such cases only from old friends. But the Clarken marriage had always been the best. The couple had met only four or five years before, both of them reasonably mature career people. Jane had had her own life as a secretary to one of the highest-placed men in the Senate. She had given that up for Dave and had been candid, last Christmas, about their plans for a child this year. If there had been a crackup, it had come with devastating quickness.

"Is she all right?" Rush asked.

"She's fine," Clarken said. "She isn't ill, anything like that. But something is . . . going on, Milo. Jesus, I've got to talk to somebody!"

"Look, then, buddy. Lay it on me. I love both of you characters. You know that."

Clarken nodded, his eyes haunted. "I know that."

"Then lay it on me."

"When I came home the night before last, something had happened. I don't know what. She was all . . . upset. Her eyes looked as though she had been crying."

"Did you ask her about it?"

"Yes, but she said nothing was wrong."

"All right." Rush leaned back, waiting.

"Yesterday I tried to call her twice about lunchtime, and the line was busy. Then I called back a little later and there was no answer. When I asked her about it, she said she had been shopping all over the District."

"Anything wrong with that?"

Clarken's face twisted. "I had just had her car serviced. I happened to have the mileage on the work order. I—shit, this sounds really bad—I checked her speedometer. She couldn't have been out shopping. She hadn't put a single mile on the clock."

"She could have gone shopping with someone else, but I assume you thought of that, so there must be more."

"She's not acting right, Milo. You know how sunny she always is . . . how she's always so happy, so forthright, and she's always acted like—like she loves the hell out of me. But she's all shook up. Half the idle talk she made at dinner last night didn't even make good sense. It was as if she were going through the motions but she wasn't even *there*. And then last night I woke up in the middle of the night and she was awake. I could hear the way she was breathing. She was just lying there, awake. She never does that. She never acts like this. When I tried to talk to her about it, she just shut me off, said I was imagining it all. Then today I went home for lunch. I don't do that ordinarily, but I was worried about her. I thought maybe we could talk it out, whatever it is. She wasn't there. The mail had come. There was this brown envelope, addressed to her. It looked funny, not like an ad. It was sort of heavy." Clarken took a shuddering breath. "Well, I opened the goddamned thing."

It was familiar in scope if not in details, and inwardly Rush tightened himself for whatever was to come. The pattern he knew too well: the doubt, the sudden erosion of trust, and then the beginnings of transgressions against each other's rights and privacy that were often worse than whatever it might be that was suspected. Rush said nothing.

"There were pictures," Clarken said.

"Of Jane?"

"Of her and this . . . man. Resort pictures, you know, that kind of thing. Eight-by-ten glossies of her and this . . . guy. They were having a hell of a time, by the pictures. I don't know who he is. I can't even tell when the pictures were taken. She hasn't changed at all, that I can see, since we've been married, and maybe her hair looked a little different in the pictures, or maybe she just had it fixed a little differently. I can't tell. I couldn't tell. I studied them. I couldn't make out whether they were old pictures or recent pictures. But goddamn it, there they were, these pictures somebody had sent her, *to our house*, and I don't know if she's got something going with somebody, or somebody is blackmailing her, or what the hell is going on."

"You figure the pictures have to be tied up with her mood?"

"Oh, shit, I know it."

"What did you do with the pictures?"

"I put them back in the envelope and put all the mail back in the mailbox, just as if I hadn't been home."

"She'll see that the envelope was torn open."

"No, it was one of those with a metal fastener that I just bent open, and the flap pulled apart on the glue line. She won't know."

"Why did you do that, Dave?"

"Because I didn't know what else to do!"

"What are you going to do now?" Rush was being patient, trying to find a way.

Clarken shook his head. "I don't know, man. If I try to talk to her about it, I have to admit I opened her mail. But if I don't say anything, and it just keeps on—" He stopped right there.

"The only thing in the world to do is talk to her about it, Dave."

"No. I just can't do that."

"You're upset and so is she. You need to get it out into the open."

Clarken raised pale, haunted eyes. "You have an investigator in your office. What if you had him watch her?"

"Oh, Dave."

"Make it a regular business deal. I'll pay you a retainer."

"Dave, for Christ's sake!"

"All right, it's crazy. You think I'm crazy."

"I don't think you're crazy."

"Then what if you saw her? What if you, say, came by the house as if to see me tomorrow afternoon, and I made it a point to be out?"

"What would that accomplish?"

"Well, you could . . . see how you think she looks. You could possibly get a reading of some kind."

Rush sighed. "Why don't *you* get a reading? Why don't you *ask?*"

"Milo, goddamn it, we're friends, aren't we?"

"I'm Jane's friend, too."

"Well, then, what's wrong with your coming by the house? Maybe she wants somebody else to talk to. Maybe you'd be doing her a favor. I'm not asking you to spy on her or anything. I just think, if you went by, you might get some impression."

"Dave," Rush said sadly, "you're not talking sense."

"I don't know about sense. I'm just asking you to do this for me. As a friend."

Rush thought about it. It was not a happy choice, because

whatever he did now, something or someone was compromised.

Clarken said, "It won't hurt you to go by and talk with her. That's all I'm asking."

"I don't see what it can accomplish."

"Will you do it? Please?"

"Dave, it's stupid!"

"Will you do it or not?"

Friendship sometimes required strange things. Milo Rush was not pleased, but the quality of desperation in Clarken's manner could not be ignored.

"I'll drop by tomorrow, Dave, if that's what you want me to do."

Saturday afternoon, Milo Rush drove to College Park. The Clarkens lived in a small but attractive one-floor plan on a curved street lined with trees. Jane Clarken's Nova was parked in the maple-shaded driveway. Rush parked behind it.

Jane answered the door chime. She was a tall girl, startlingly beautiful, with her blond hair loose on her back in the youthful fashion. She was wearing shorts and a halter, pale blue. For just an instant, before there was recognition, Rush saw the tension in her vivid green eyes. Then she smiled.

"Milo. How nice. Come in."

Rush stepped into the small flagstone foyer leading down into the contemporary living room that overlooked a tree-studded garden. The house was still and sleek and modern and cool. "I was in the neighborhood," he said.

Jane came down the two shallow steps into the living room, moving with the grace of a ballerina. "Dave is at the office, I'm afraid."

"On Saturday afternoon?"

"He is a glutton. Would you like a drink? I'm having lemonade."

"That sounds fine. It's hot out there."

Jane Clarken made a face. "August is always hot in Washington."

Rush watched her closely as she brought the lemonade from the small corner bar. She seemed pale despite her lustrous tan, as if a sudden brief illness had given her an unhealthy color beneath the skin. She was calm, however, and in control. Rush felt foolish.

She sat in a chair facing the couch, crossing beautiful legs. "Now let's hear the latest exploits of the famed attorney."

Rush grimaced. "Let's hear the exploits of the Clarken family instead."

"We're always the same, Milo. We've just been having a quiet summer."

"Is Dave okay?"

"Working too hard, of course."

"And you?"

She reached for her Kents on the end table. Her fingers shook ever so slightly. She snapped her lighter and inhaled smoke. "Couldn't be better," she said. "Of course."

"You have a slight case of nerves," Rush observed gently.

Her laugh seemed brittle. "The dog-days jitters."

"Is that what it is?"

"I suppose so. I've been thinking about getting away for a day or two. One of my girlfriends is going shopping in New York. I may go along."

Rush smiled. "New York in August is not a paradise."

"It's different, though."

"Dave going with you?"

"No, just my friend and me."

"Trial separations," Rush observed mildly, "are a terrible phenomenon."

She laughed, and there was a trace of the old roguishness in her eyes. "The day *we* have a trial separation—"

The telephone in the foyer sounded. She literally jumped. The change in her expression for the briefest moment was startling. It was fear.

She recovered. "Excuse me."

Rush remained on the couch as she went to the foyer. He could hear the rich timbre of her voice, lowered, but could not make out words. In the backyard, birds hopped along the lawn, pecking. A squirrel scolded from the branch of a locust tree. In the room, with its cathedral ceiling, everything was cool, well ordered and right. Jane Clarken's taste in furniture ran to white leather and rich dark reds and blues. The paintings on the walls were originals, quiet abstracts with suggestions of figures within them. There was a fireplace and a color television set; a wicker wine rack, stocked with good domestics, stood beside the bar.

Rush was actually thirty-eight, but his prematurely gray hair contrasted with his athletic build to cause some people to guess his age wrong by as much as ten years in either direction. For the last ten years he had been one of the nation's top half-dozen trial lawyers, and, among the independents, probably number one. Among the skills he had acquired was the ability to judge people. He knew now, without systematic analysis, that Dave Clarken had not been imagining things. Something was wrong.

Jane Clarken was no fool. She was covering reasonably well. But she was under enormous pressure of some sort. Her laugh was not quite spontaneous, her eyes did not meet his in the usual direct way, her nerves were strung painfully taut. She was not merely worried. She was afraid of something . . . someone.

Rush tried to imagine how he could proceed to be of help. He felt slightly baffled.

Jane came back into the room. "That was Davey. He said the first time in a year you come by unannounced, and he has to be stuck at the office."

"Ah, he's still there, then?"

"He said to tell you he's thinking of taking up some undemanding job, such as the practice of law."

"I can hear him saying that," Rush said, smiling.

"More lemonade?"

"I'm fine, thanks."

She sat down again.

"Dave's happy these days?" Rush asked casually.

"Oh, yes."

"And you?"

Her eyes crinkled in a smile that was almost just right. "Yes."

"Good."

"Why did you ask that way, Milo?"

He shrugged. "No reason."

She cupped her hands over a raised knee. "Tell me about the Schenbeckler case."

They talked for a while. Rush did not press his inquiry. When the time seemed appropriate, he announced it was time for him to leave. Jane made token protests, but it was clear that she was not really sorry to see him go. Rush sensed the strain she was under to act normal in the face of the pressure of whatever was going on.

At the front door he turned to her. "We don't see each other very often, but that doesn't mean our friendship is any less strong."

"I know," she said, smiling.

"And if either of you ever needs anything," Rush said carefully, "I am available."

Her eyes changed, got very bright, as if she were going to cry. "I know that, too."

"You remember it."

She nodded and turned away quickly.

Driving into the District to his office, Milo Rush reviewed the scant evidence and tried to think of a logical next step he might take. He knew now that Dave Clarken had not been imagining things, and he wondered about the pictures. If it had been some sort of blackmail attempt, he thought Jane would have confided in him. It seemed highly unlikely, if not impossible, that she was hiding an affair. Jane was one of the moderns, very much out front with everything. If there had been a lover, it was much more likely that she would have coolly informed Dave about it, told him it was just a stage she had to get through, and asked for his patience. And in that kind of situation, Dave, the poor bastard, would have writhed—and waited for her to tire of her new playmate.

But it was not like that, Rush concluded. As unlikely as such a thing seemed in this time and place, Dave and Jane Clarken had an ideal relationship that was working, one based on genuine love. Whatever was going on was something else. Rush hoped he was wrong, for once, in his gut feeling that it was something sinister.

Not long after he reached his office, Dave Clarken called. Rush shared the little information he had garnered and again suggested confronting Jane about the photographs. Clarken sounded more worried, but said he would think about it.

On Sunday afternoon, Clarken called Rush at his apartment. She was talking about going to New York, shopping, Clarken said. Was this unusual? No, but Clarken did not like it, somehow. Had he admitted this? Yes, he had told her that he didn't want her to go this time. There had been a brief argument. Had he mentioned the pictures? No. Did he plan to do so, and get it out into the open? Clarken did not know. He sounded strung out.

On Monday, Rush flew his Piper Arrow to Philadelphia for a deposition hearing. Traffic and weather were both heavy in the Washington area, and it was nightfall when he checked his answering service from the airport. There was a call from Dave Clarken on the list, and the girl said Clarken had told her it was an extreme emergency.

Using the telephone booth beside the brightly lighted bustle of the Flight Service Station, Rush dialed Clarken's home number. Dave Clarken answered on the first ring.

"Dave? Milo Rush."

"Milo . . . she's gone . . ."

Three

LESTER MONTGOMERY strode into Milo Rush's office, dropped into one of the leather chairs facing the desk, lighted a huge black cigar, and fanned the match. He was a tall, golden-haired man who looked a little like Jack Nicklaus, though younger.

"What's the caper?" he asked briskly.

Milo Rush winced.

"What?" Montgomery said.

"Role-playing is a terrible thing," Rush told him.

"You said we had an investigative problem, big daddy."

"That doesn't mean you have to come in here talking like Perry Mason."

Montgomery got to his feet. "You want I should go out and come in again?"

"Sit down, you dummy."

"Man, I can't seem to please you today!"

Rush scanned the few hasty notes on his desk. "At the moment, this is a missing person case. The police have not been notified—"

"I thought we didn't do this kind of stuff anymore."

"This is a friend."

"Male or female?" Montgomery had his notebook on his knee.

"Female."

"Hubba hubba."

"Will you please cool it?"

23

"Okay, okay."

"The name is Jane Clarken—Mrs. David. Maiden name: Riley. Five feet six. About a hundred and twenty pounds. Hair: blond, long. Eyes: green. Here's a recent snapshot. Home address and some additional data are written on the back."

Montgomery eyed the Polaroid, which showed Jane in a swimsuit beside a pool. Montgomery's eyes widened. "As I said—"

"I don't believe she's still in the city," Rush cut in. "She might have gone to New York. She did not go in her own car, but she could have gone in someone else's. She left her home address sometime between noon and three o'clock yesterday, Monday. She took a blue overnight case and a change of clothes."

"Marriage fallout?"

"I don't think so, Les."

"What, then?"

"I really have no idea."

Montgomery studied the photo. "She a friend of yours, or her husband?"

"Both, if I understand your syntax."

"No cops, though."

"That is correct."

"You got a list of credit cards?"

Rush handed over the brief list that Dave Clarken had provided.

Montgomery pocketed the paper. "Taxi dispatchers might be a place to start. Then I'll get on the other angles. I might have something for you by tomorrow afternoon."

"I want it *this* afternoon, Les."

"Are you forgetting the Bishop hearing?"

"No, I'm not forgetting anything."

"It's an important hearing, Milo. I'm prepped for it."

"Tell Sam to take it."

"Sam doesn't know enough about it."

"Then get a postponement."

The last traces of Montgomery's facetiousness vanished. "Yes, sir."

Rush softened his tone. "I didn't mean to jump down your

throat. But this is pretty high priority as far as I'm concerned."

Montgomery nodded seriously. "I'll get right on it."

"If you locate her, I don't want her contacted. I want to be told, that's all."

"All right."

"And if this runs into the police at any point, you're to back off and let me know that, too. Immediately."

Montgomery put the photo in his pocket with his notebook and list. "She's a friend of yours, so is her husband, she walked off from her house yesterday early in the afternoon, you don't think it's marital trouble, and the police haven't been notified. Right?"

Milo Rush nodded.

"I don't get it," Montgomery said.

"I don't either."

"Hubba," Montgomery said thoughtfully, "hubba." And walked out.

The intercom light flashed. Rush touched the button. "Yes?"

Marty, his secretary, said, "May I see you a moment?"

"Okay."

Rush waited. It was Marty's signal that someone was in the outer office. By coming in, she announced the visitor privately, so that excuses could be made when necessary without being overheard. Glancing at his watch, Rush thought he knew who was waiting.

His secretary, a pretty redhead, came through the private door. She carried some envelopes and documents which she placed on his desk. "Mr. Clarken is waiting."

"Fine. Send him in. No calls while he's here."

"I have this check from the chemical company. Do you want it in the regular account?"

"How much is it?"

"Ten thousand."

"No, uh, why don't you send it to the brokerage account, Marty?"

"Mister Beaveridge will have a fit."

"Well, Mister Beaveridge is an accountant. They're paid to have fits. Just make a notation and send it on."

"This isn't their complete fee payment."

"I know, but they're a big outfit. They get to take their time paying their bills."

She smiled. "Unlike the common folk." She was a very fetching young woman, and her yellow dress did things that were really unnecessary for her. She turned to walk to the door, moving demurely.

"What do I have on for lunch?" Rush asked her.

"Mr. Patterson."

"Will you cancel that, please?"

She turned, surprised. "At one, you have arguments in the—"

"Tell Sandy he'll have to handle that alone, will you? And what do I have on later?"

"You have *me* on later. I hope you're not going to cancel me, too."

"Marty," Rush sighed, "I don't know if we'll see that play or not."

She looked at him directly. "That part of the evening I can forgo, Mr. Rush, sir."

"We'll just have to wait and see how this meeting goes, Marty."

She looked at him some more.

He said, "Maybe it will work out."

"I hope so," she said softly.

Rush leaned back in his leather chair and closed his eyes for a moment after she had left. He had the beginnings of a dull headache. He thought about the crowded calendar that was being wrecked and the evening that was possibly going to be wrecked as well. He hadn't had any time with Marty for almost a month. At the office it was always business, and briskly efficient, as it had to be. He remembered the last time at her apartment, the dusky glow of her body as the pale green gown slid to the floor. His pulse moved sluggishly.

The reception door opened and Dave Clarken came in. He had shaved, and his clothes were fresh, but he looked haggard. He shook hands with the instinctive fervor of an emergency. "Do you know anything yet, Milo?"

"It's too early yet, Dave. Sit down. I'm going to fix you a drink."

Clarken sat down. "I don't drink at this time of day."

"You're drinking today." Rush opened the wall panel.

"I called all our friends. No one has heard from her. I felt like a damned fool. I think they must have thought I was hysterical, trying to act like nothing was wrong. Can you imagine how I sounded?—'Hello, this is Dave Clarken, and I wonder if you've seen Jane. No, nothing is wrong. She just seems to have gone visiting somewhere, and I . . .' Oh, Christ!"

Rush handed him Jack Daniel's on the rocks. "Drink that like a good boy. Nobody had heard from her?"

Clarken bolted part of the bourbon and shuddered. "No. And no one was going to New York. The last two times she went shopping in New York, it was with Jill Phillips. Jill said they had talked about going the end of the month, but not now. Nobody was going *now*."

Milo Rush recognized the signs of a sleepless night and galloping hysteria. He kept his tone as dispassionate as possible. "Let's just reconstruct a little, shall we?"

"I told you the whole thing. There's nothing to go over."

"Well, humor me. We'll just review it briefly, to make sure nothing has been overlooked, all right?"

Clarken took another bolt of Jack Daniel's and nodded, the glass clutched in his locked hands.

"In the first place, you did not bring up the matter of the pictures. Is that right?"

"That's right. I didn't know what to say—"

"All right. Fine. There was no argument?"

"No!"

"You saw her Monday morning?"

"Yesterday morning? Yes. She got up. She fixed my breakfast. She usually does. That's normal. Everything was normal. She was . . . nervous, maybe, but nothing you could make an issue of. Just a little tense, maybe. But we didn't fight or anything. I thought maybe *she* wasn't really tense at all, but it was all *me*, worrying about those photographs and everything."

Rush nodded. "Then you called at noon."

"Yes. She wasn't there, as I told you. But the cleaning lady was in, and she said Jane had run to the grocery for a few things.

She—the cleaning lady—said she was just leaving, she said she'd leave a note saying I had called."

"But Jane didn't return your call, and you—"

"I got to thinking about what you said about joining a club or something." Clarken grimaced. "I thought, my God, you know, we hadn't been playing much. I thought, well, you know, maybe she was just bored out of her mind, and if she was fooling around with somebody, well . . . we hadn't been going out much or anything and maybe it was innocent, and what I ought to do was try to get myself organized better, join a club or something like that. I thought I'd go home early and we'd go out and look at a couple of clubs, the two of us. Maybe not a country club but a yacht club. You know how she loves the water. . . . So I got off early, just said the hell with it, and went home. And there was her car and there was the empty house and there was her note."

Rush glanced down at his desk. The note, in Jane's fine handwriting, was among the papers there.

> Darling,
>
> This is really a rotten thing to do on such short notice, but I have a chance to make that NY shopping spree and I'm just rushing out the door to go DO it before my nerves frazzle completely. There's nothing wrong. Please don't worry or be upset. I know it's weird (sp?) but I just have to get off to myself for a few days. Be back Sunday latest. I love you.
>
> Jane

"She doesn't *do* things like that," Clarken said huskily.

"I know," Rush agreed.

"The note makes no sense anyway. She could have called."

"I know."

"And it's a lie, I mean she doesn't mention the pictures, and they've got something to do with it!"

"Did you bring the pictures?" Rush asked.

Clarken's eyes widened. "No!"

Rush was puzzled. "Didn't I ask you to look for them?"

"Yes."

"And did you?"

"Yes, but I didn't find them. She must have done something

with them. Maybe she took them with her. Maybe she hid them too well. I don't know. But it doesn't matter, does it? I told you what they were. You don't have to see them."

"All right," Rush said, getting to his feet. "End of interview."

Clarken looked up, startled. "What?"

"I said—"

"Isn't there anything more to talk about? Any more information—"

"Dave, I'm going to try to help you. Jane's gone, and it takes no great feat of intelligence to recognize that her letter is about as honest as a Pentagon press release. It's damned strange. I'm concerned. But what makes you think I'm willing to sit here and waste my time listening to you lie to me?"

"I'm not lying! I—"

"Bullshit." Rush used the word softly, like a club.

Clarken stared at him.

"You're lying about the pictures," Rush told him. "I don't know whether you found them or not, but you're lying about them in some regard. Lies just aren't that hard to spot sometimes. So let's just forget it, Dave. I'll do what I can for you, and you just hide all the information you want, and if Jane is in trouble, and your information might have helped—"

"All right," Clarken said. "All *right*."

Rush, standing beside his desk in an attitude of departure, waited. He did not like being forced to deal with Dave this way.

Clarken hung his head. "I *can't* find the damned photographs. Maybe she burned them. I *hope* she burned the goddamned things."

Carefully, Rush said nothing.

"You wouldn't want to see them," Clarken whispered, his face down. "I wouldn't show them to you or anybody. They were—oh, God, I don't know—they were *party* pictures, you know? I mean, they were all taken in a room somewhere, a big bedroom or something with fancy Victorian-style furniture and everything, and there were about six people in them . . . Jane and two other girls, and these three men. And they're all . . . they're stripped down . . . dancing . . . on the bed . . . having drinks . . . and Jane is—Jane is the center of attraction in a lot of them, and there's a sequence—there were more pictures than I said, maybe twenty in all, and there's this one, this guy . . . the son of a bitch is lying on his back on the floor, and Jane is . . . she's on her hands and knees, over him, and there's this other guy behind her, and he's—while she's doing this one thing, the other guy is . . . while he's—"

"All right, Dave," Rush said quickly, shocked.

"They've *got* to be old pictures. They couldn't be new. It has to be something out of her past, you know? But I couldn't tell. She's just the same now in appearance, but she wouldn't do that *now*—but I never thought she would *ever* be in that kind of a thing, with those goddamned sons of bitches—" Clarken broke down.

It was very much unexpected, this information, and Milo Rush did not quite know how to cope with it. He was not naïve, but he would never have placed Jane in a situation like that. And yet, instantly, as he tried to absorb the data, he found himself remembering how Jane had looked in her living room on Saturday. She was so beautiful and so alive. There had been other times in the past, he thought, when it had jarred him to learn that a beautiful woman was stupid, or corrupt. Men liked their visions whole.

Had he made that male chauvinist-style mistake with Jane Clarken? Had he *assumed* a decency in her because she was so lovely? And underneath, had she been . . .

He got that far and rejected the possibility.

No, he knew better.

But if the pictures existed, as they did, they said things about her either now or in the past that neither he nor Dave had guessed. And if *he* was stunned, what did this evidence mean to Dave?

Crumpled in the chair, Clarken made ugly sounds such as a man makes when he fights a grief that will get out. Whatever happened now, a violence had been done. He would never see his wife again without remembering the photographs. And no one could say now what this would mean.

Milo Rush put his hand awkwardly on Clarken's shoulder. "All right, Dave," he said softly. "All right, old son. All right." Which of course did no good whatsoever.

She was silent beside him as Joe Graeber drove out of the airport grounds and into traffic. As she had always been, she was cool, with an almost startling immaculate quality. Her hair was perfectly done up, there was no sign of a wrinkle in her white slacks and blouse, and her white sandals looked absolutely new, fitting her nyloned feet exquisitely. She had always had this quality of perfection, and Graeber, in his rumpled blue pants and garish sport shirt, felt the old pulse of irritated desire. He could smell his own sweat despite the car's air conditioning, and he wondered how it would be to muss her up, tear down the cool exterior and make her writhe against the wetness of his skin. There had always been a pain-pleasure in sending her on an assignment, knowing that if he could not afford her directly, he could force her degradation with someone else. He had always liked it best when he sent her to spoil herself on someone she would find repulsive. It had been a long time, but the old pleasure was still there.

"Don't worry about the suitcase," he told her. "It just went to St. Louis. You'll have it by evening."

"I'm sure there's a shop," she said, not looking at him.

"You better believe it. And you need to spend a little of that wad for appearance's sake anyhow."

She said nothing, looking straight ahead, maddeningly aloof.

"After all," Graeber told her, "you're here to get over your recent bereavement, right? You want to forget, right? You're loaded, right?"

"Right," she said wearily.

"I got you a Thunderbird. You ought to like that."

She said nothing.

"I got you a room overlooking the pool."

She looked straight ahead as if he were not there.

"Anything else you want," Graeber said, goaded, "all you got to do is say so."

She lighted a cigarette and managed to make even this act seem elegant.

"Can you think of anything?" Graeber asked.

"No," she said.

"It's not like you had to screw him," Graeber exploded. "That's entirely up to you. A lot of women would give their ass to have this kind of a holiday, everything paid. If you screw him, that's your business. I can't help it if you've got your best weapon between your legs."

She turned to him. "God, you're a pig."

"A pig? Right. You better believe I'm a pig, you little whore. I'm just the pig who made the Dominican Republic operation go. I'm just the pig who got you out of it, clear, when the Sandresko deal blew up. You better believe I'm a pig. I'm the pig with the camera, right?"

Her face set, she stared straight ahead through the windshield.

"Right?" Graeber prodded.

"Right," she said very softly.

"So you just remember it."

They drove through the traffic toward the downtown area, she coolly elegant, Graeber stewing in his own juices. She was so beautiful and distant, and Graeber's level of controlled desperation so intense, that he briefly considered driving her to a motel, taking her inside and raping her, finally, just once for the record. He knew, however, that he could not afford such luxury. He had already pushed her as far as she would go. He needed her for this job. Badly.

The way he hated her was a very special thing. She had always been so much better than he, letting him know without ever saying a word. And yet he had always been the one in charge. He was the one with the expertise, the one who took the risks. And she had come out of it unscathed, while he had taken all the lumps. Now he was scrambling and she had practically everything, was out of the life, married, living in luxury. It was not fair.

But he had gotten her back, for this. He still had the power over her, and it felt good. After this operation, he would not need her anymore. He would be back on top. He would have the money he needed. There would be other jobs. There were always plenty of jobs for a man of his abilities if the recent record was one of success. Then she could go to hell, he told himself.

He drove on downtown, found the parking garage, a stack of concrete waffles on a street near a railroad track, and drove inside. The attendant recognized him and let him drive himself up to the fourth level. The T-Bird was there, dark red, gleaming. Graeber parked beside it.

Bursting into a fresh sweat in the murky under-roof heat, he transferred her suitcase and cosmetic bag to the Ford. He unlocked the driver's side door and held it, with mocking formality, as she slid behind the wheel. He handed her the keys. She tried the engine. It thrummed. Air conditioning hissed. She put the gear selector in reverse and looked up at him.

"There's a map in the glove box if you need it," he told her.

"All right."

"I'll be in touch tomorrow by phone. You'll see me around the place Thursday. You have everything straight?"

She nodded. The brake lights of the Thunderbird blinked as she released, then reapplied the brakes. She was anxious to go, to get away from him.

Graeber softened. "Look, baby," he muttered, touching her shoulder. "I *need* this help; right? This is really important. I wouldn't have asked you otherwise."

She looked up at him, her face twisting in revulsion, and moved so that his hand slipped off her shoulder. She could have slapped him and hurt less.

Graeber stepped back. "Okay. Move it."

"You'll call tomorrow?"

"That's affirmative," he said stiffly.

She backed the car out of the slot, put it in drive, and went down the curving ramp, out of sight. Graeber could hear the tires shrilling on a lower level as she drove hard. He was gritting his teeth in frustration. He had the taste of blood in his mouth.

"Okey dokey, bubba," Les Montgomery said wearily. "I got the poop, but I don't think you are going to be entranced by its implications."

Milo Rush put the chicken salad sandwich down on his desk beside the glass of scotch. It was almost 8 P.M. and he was tired and disgusted. "Tell me," he suggested.

Montgomery shuffled the pages of his notebook. He had been going all day, with periodic telephone calls from all over the city, and had had some help from a retired police detective they sometimes used. He looked as weary as Rush felt.

"First of all, the lady has come into a wad of cash money. Don't ask me where."

Rush nodded. "That's why the credit card investigation got us nowhere."

"Yep. Cash, all cash."

"Do you know where she *is?*"

"Not exactly. But I got a pretty good idea. You want conclusions first, or sequentially?"

Rush leaned back and put his feet up. "Hell, just get on with it any way you want."

"She took a cab from her house. She went downtown. She went to the TWA ticket office. She had the cab wait. Then she had him take her to a shop called Pinocchio's."

"I never heard of it," Rush said.

"Right. Neither had the driver. He had to call in to ask directions. She didn't know exactly where it was either, which seemed funny to him, helped him remember. Anyway, it's one of those new places, very exclusive. It leans toward clothes for milady that have some sex. Not blatant, but definitely not conservative. Our cabbie dumped her there."

"What did she buy?"

"Damned near the whole store." Montgomery consulted a list. "Two shorts outfits, nineteen for one, twenty-two for the other; one tennis dress, ninety-six bucks; two bikinis; four pairs of shoes; three pairs of slacks; two pullovers; one halter; two sun dresses; one purse; one evening gown, long; one summer suit; one nylon blouse; one hat." Montgomery made a face. "Underwear, nylons, cosmetics, a ton of stuff. And two suitcases and a cosmetic bag to haul it all off in. Fourteen hundred and eighty-one dollars and twenty-one cents. Cash."

"She didn't have that kind of money in her account."

"She didn't write a check. She peeled off the folding money. She told the people at the store she was going to Europe and her husband had told her to splurge."

"Did she use her own name? I assume they wanted to be sure they knew where they could send ads."

"She used her maiden name, Riley, and the address of a gas station."

Rush was puzzled. "Then what?"

"New cab ride. The driver remembers the ton of packages. Down to the Mayflower. Check in. Go upstairs. Unwrap all the stuff, pack it in the suitcases, leave all the boxes and stuff, check out again."

"This was all yesterday?"

"Right."

"Then what?"

"There's a hole of an hour or two, but about dark she was at the airport, picking up her ticket. She got on a TWA for Columbus."

"Ohio?"

"Yep."

"Was she alone on the plane?"

"She was ticketed singly. For whatever that's worth."

"Nothing," Rush grunted.

"She changed names for the airplane," Montgomery volunteered. "She winged her solitary way westward as Mrs. Walter Hendrix."

"Does that name mean anything?"

"It's the name of one of her friends who's sitting at home in Chevy Chase knowing nothing about nothing, not even that her name has been taken in vain."

Rush closed his eyes and thought about it. The headache, a day-long companion, nudged at the inside of his skull.

Montgomery said, "If you want my opinion, bubba, I think she's got a playmate."

"I don't think so," Rush said.

"It all points that way."

"There are a few details you don't know."

"Goodie. Fill me in."

Rush ignored the request. "Tell you what. Get the next flight out for Columbus. See if there's anything at all you can turn up there. I'll be home later tonight. Call me."

Montgomery's forehead wrinkled. "Chances are pretty slim."

"I know that. Try."

"We're beginning to run up a lot of expenses."

"I shudder. Get going."

Montgomery sighed and left.

Milo Rush finished his meager supper, downed the scotch,

thought about it awhile, and then called Dave Clarken and gave him some, but not all, of the details.

Clarken's voice shook. "She isn't doing this voluntarily, Milo."

"There's no sign of force, Dave."

"I think I should notify the police."

"No."

"Why?"

"Dave, no one has taken her off by force."

"The pictures, though. If someone is coercing her—"

"Do you want to tell the police about the pictures?"

"Oh, Christ."

"I've got a man working on it," Rush told his friend. "Try to get some sleep. You sound a little ragged. I'll be in touch just as soon as we have more word."

"I ought to pay you something," Clarken said. "Isn't a retainer fee customary? I don't know anything about deals like this, but if I ought to pay you some money—"

"We'll worry about it later."

"I don't want to take advantage of you," Clarken said earnestly. "If I should send a fee or something now, to your office, tell me."

Rush thought about the usual fee for work of this nature, then compared it with Clarken's nervous need to be reassured that all was normal. "You could mail a check for a couple of hundred," he said. "That ought to cover it."

Next he called Marty.

"Can you?" she asked. She sounded a little breathless.

"I'm sorry, babe."

"Shit, shit, shit!"

It was 2:10 A.M. when Les Montgomery called, on a bad connection, from Columbus. "The age of miracles hasn't passed, bubba!"

"What have you got?"

"TWA lost one of her bags. It went to St. Louis by mistake. It's back now, but she left the Hendrix name and a forwarding address for the bag."

"God bless TWA," Rush said. "What's the forwarding address?"

"Kenton's Run."

"What in the hell is that?"

Montgomery sounded amused. "Well, it seems there was this famous Indian-fighter feller, name of Simon Kenton, who came down the Ohio River long time ago—"

"Les. What is Kenton's Run?"

"It's a swanky resort down in southern Ohio where the elite meet to eat, or beat their meat, or I don't know. But anyhow, it's this place where good old Simon Kenton was supposed to have run a hundred yelping savages into the ground, and the resort is supposed to be a dandy."

"And our Mrs. Walter Hendrix is there?"

"Her bag is going out there in the morning, bubba. And what do you bet she's there, waiting for it?"

If it had been anyone else but Jane Clarken—or if the photographs had not entered into the evidence—Rush would have washed his hands of it. But there was a bad feeling to the details, a crazy inconsistency, that tugged at the edges of his mind. Despite how much of it looked, Rush detected the sour smell of genuine trouble.

At 3 A.M. he left a message for Dave Clarken on the office recorder, leaving out all reference to where Jane might be and bending over backward to try to be reassuring.

At 5 A.M. he took off from Washington in his private plane, turning west and setting up the omnirange receiver for the first radio beacon on a course to Columbus, Ohio.

Four

THE history of southeastern Ohio is interesting. The Indians had tacit title to parts of it later than some other sections because the severe roll of its terrain did not make it wildly attractive to farming-oriented settlers. A portion of it was used to swindle immigrants lured by the promise of free land. Later, large areas were stripped of their native hardwood timber, farmed stupidly, and left in ruin. The WPA planted millions of pine seedlings; silly, critics said, but the pine trees started to grow, and a few native plants crept back in. Years passed. Ohioans on dime-store vacations visited impressive rock formations, foliage-shrouded canyons, and caves. Farmers learned how to grow better crops on the hillsides and the closed little valleys. The area remained behind the rest of the state in population density and other aspects of development. The roads are mostly narrow and twisting and two-lane. The farms are spread, tucked in here and there between lumpy hills topped by monk's cap woods. By day, the broken horizons are indistinctly blue-gray from a gentle humidity, and at night, in the summer, the temperature drops quickly and cool fog creeps out of the woods and across the fields.

Kenton's Run had been built in a remote area once worked over by the WPA, and the curving road had been cut through a dense pine forest. Coming to the bottom of a steep, twisting section of road, Milo Rush cranked the wheel of the rented Chevvie hard to the right, fed the engine gasoline to climb a startlingly slanted way back up, turned around a rock formation, swept along a long, gentle curve where guard rails suddenly appeared, and got a glimpse of the lodge ahead and below.

It was tucked into one of those tree-filled valleys. A small lake showed blue-green through trees beyond. Cars glittered in a parking lot. It looked, unbelievably, like a small hotel in the North Miami Beach area: a concrete-and-glass half-moon, layered like a parking garage, white, with flags flying on top.

"Hubba hubba," Les Montgomery said.

"That's not," Rush winced, "how I would have put it."

"It really fits in nice, man. Like a turd in a punchbowl."

They drove down to it and parked in a line of cars on pavement made furnace-hot by the bright sun. By prearrangement Rush carried his suitcase toward the front entrance, while Montgomery strolled along the front sidewalk, planning a circuit of the grounds.

There was a pool in the shade of the front entrance. It had star-shaped sprinkler heads made of anodized aluminum and a lot of lights for after-dark effects. There were no fish. It smelled strongly of chlorine.

In the air-conditioned interior, red carpet and paneling and leather furniture predominated. The lobby was strung out to accommodate small shops, mostly deserted. The long registration counter was empty, too, except for one man who was arguing with the two pretty girls behind it. Rush walked up quietly.

The man at the far end was heavy-set, and his face was red with anger. He had picked up a heavy chunk of black glass, used to hold announcement cards, and was thunking it dully against the formica counter. "I don't give a goddamn about the Jenson meetings or anything else," he said too loudly. "My wife and I made these reservations six weeks ago, and we want a room that looks toward the lake."

The two girls looked grim—concerned, but helpless. "I'm sorry, sir," the brunette, who looked a little older, said. "It's the best we have."

Leaning sideways on the counter, the man hadn't seen Rush at this far end yet. "I want to see the manager."

"The manager went to town, sir, but he'll be—"

"I want to see who's in charge."

"I'm in charge while the manager is out, sir, but—"

"I want a goddamned room looking out on the goddamned lake!"

"Sir, I'm *sorry*. We—"

Muttering an expletive, the man swung his right arm, which held the heavy glass paperweight. He let it go, zinging it down the length of the counter with great velocity, like a puck.

Milo Rush stuck out his hand and caught it before it could crash into the mirror tiles on the wall. The man turned and saw him for the first time.

"You dropped something," Rush said, shooting the chunk of glass back down the counter six times harder than it had come. It hit the man in the midsection and dropped with a thud to the carpet.

The man started to say something. His mouth worked. The missile had hurt. It was hard to tell which startled him more: the counterattack, or the realization that someone else had come along and he didn't have the two women to bully by himself.

He licked his lips and pointed a shaky finger at the brunette. "I want to see the manager as soon as he gets back."

"Yes, sir."

He lurched away and headed for the coffee shop sign.

The two girls smiled covertly at each other, and the brunette came over to where Rush was standing. Friendliness brightened her eyes. "Yes, sir?"

"I wanted a room," Rush told her. "But it sounds like I'm out of luck."

"Board or management, sir?"

"What?"

"Are you with the Jenson group?"

"No, I'm not."

She shook her head in apology. "We have a large business meeting beginning in the morning, and I assumed you were part of that group."

"Does that mean no rooms for anybody else?"

"Oh, no. They have two floors."

Rush read her name tag. "Then there are some rooms open, Jenny?"

She smiled with her eyes, said without turning, "Lora, will you

40

bring the keys to two twenty-six?" She placed a registration blank on the counter. "I think you'll like it, sir. It's on the lake side."

The room was large, with white walls, white carpet, black leather chairs and a cinnamon-colored bedspread. There was a dresser and a color TV set. Investigating the bathroom, Rush found that it was like a cave—black tile, black ceiling and floor, black fixtures with gold fittings. He thought briefly about the mentality that would consider it luxurious.

With the draperies open, the room afforded a fine view of the Kenton's Run complex. Near at hand was a sprawling kidney-shaped pool surrounded by a large patio and a grass-covered cabana area. Candy-striped awnings shaded small round tables. A few patrons lounged in deck chairs, watching three small boys do can-openers off the board. Two white-coated waiters brought drinks from the bar. Beyond the pool, down a slight slope, was one of the small greens of what appeared to be a tightly laid out little golf course that meandered back into the hills. Beyond the fairway was the grassy shore of the lake, where canoes and three small sailboats were moored. Looking across the small lake, Rush saw three people ambling away on horseback along a shaded trail. So there was a stable. To the right, over the roof of the cabana, the bright afternoon sun beat down on tennis courts which at the moment were deserted.

Rush unpacked his suitcase, except for the Smith and Wesson .38 which he left wrapped in a towel and securely locked. He put the suitcase in the closet. He had brought the weapon on impulse and felt melodramatic about it. It was possible there was still a logical explanation.

In a few minutes Les Montgomery tapped on the door. His face was filmy with sweat, and he went into the bathroom for a drink of water.

"Jesus Christ! The black hole of Calcutta!"

When he came out, he had turned off the monkey business. "She's here, bubba."

"Registered?"

"Mrs. Walter Hendrix. She's living in a tree house."

Rush stared at his associate.

"Back among the trees in the golf course area," Montgomery explained, "they've got these one-bedroom cabins built up on steel poles. They're really kind of clever. They call them tree houses because of the way they're built into the branches. Our lady is in number fourteen."

"Alone?"

"Yep. Disappointed?"

Rush sighed. "How do I know what to think?"

"The place is filling up. This Jenson outfit is pretty big. Seems like they're having their national sales meeting and the annual session of the board of directors simultaneously. Be about eighty, ninety sales and management types here with wives and girlfriends or whatever. Then the bigwigs."

"Do you know about Jenson? Its products or anything?"

"Well, there's a little display down there by the cabana, and it shows a goddamn airplane, so I don't know."

"I've heard of the outfit," Rush said. "They're diversified: fertilizer, golf clubs, aircraft engines."

"That ain't diversified, bubba. That's disintegrated."

"They're still fairly small and unknown, but they've gobbled up a couple of firms in the last year or two. They're coming fast."

"Our ladybug have anything to do with this meeting, you think?"

"I think," Rush said.

"Hubba hubba."

"I'd like you to find out more about Jenson," Rush said after a moment. "Key people, sales performance, dividends, options, questions before the board, if you can. Don't ask around here. There's a limousine that shuttles into Terrydale every couple hours. Ride in that way. I might need the car; you never know. Go ahead and rent yourself another one. Oh, and another thing."

He finished giving Montgomery his instructions. Montgomery nodded and left almost immediately.

Rush changed clothes. In shorts, T shirt, floppy straw hat and oversized sunglasses, he looked like the other temporary natives. He rode the elevator to the lobby with a woman of about sixty who looked a little like a stork. She was wearing two large diamond rings with her swimsuit and terrycloth robe. Her companion was a good-looking boy of about twenty. The way they stood silent in the elevator made it clear they were not family-related.

In the lobby there were more people, many in swimsuits or attire even more outlandish than Rush's protective coloration. There seemed to be a lot of children of about fourteen, overweight and bitching because there was nothing to do. Rush went to the pool.

The heat blasted him. He sat down at one of the small round tables under an umbrella. A waiter appeared with the speed of light. Rush ordered iced tea.

Most of the tables around the pool were deserted. Two lushly curved girls were baking on towels spread on the lawn nearby, and a young husband and wife grinned at each other as they sent their small child toddling back and forth between them, a distance of six feet that usually included one pratfall. A couple of older, expensively coiffed women sat carefully in the shade and sipped martinis. The kids had deserted the pool, leaving a handful of adults: an athletic-looking man, about forty, energetically using the diving board; two teen-age girls wading around up to their necks; a thirtyish-looking woman in a red one-piece suit and yellow swimming cap, more or less swimming in the shallows; and a very old doll walking around in ankle-deep water, a ridiculous two-piece swimsuit revealing all the knobs and rolls and bulges of a long life well used up.

Milo Rush kept an eye out for Jane Clarken, alias Mrs. Walter Hendrix. He also looked everybody else over for possible recognition. He smoked a cigarette and nursed the iced tea.

The woman with the bathing cap heaved herself out of the pool, dripping splendidly, and snatched up a large red towel from the pavement to wipe her face and throat. Rush watched her appreciatively from behind the sunglasses. She was of medium height and pink from the sun and a little overweight, with the suggestion of waffles on the backs of her thighs, but she had a nice, athletic, girl's body, good legs and breasts, and a round face marked by wide-set eyes that promised a sense of humor. On her, the extra weight was proof of a life being lived well, and to hell with the consequences. She peeled off the cap and let lustrous dark hair tumble onto her shoulders. The water streaming down her inner thighs made them gleam like pale velvet.

Shaking her hair, she tossed the towel over her shoulder, looked around, and came toward Milo Rush's table, walking sturdily barefooted.

"Hi there. I'm Judith Evans."

Rush smiled back at her and introduced himself.

She sat down without being asked, dripping all over everything. "Are you with this region?"

"Pardon?"

She looked at him. "You are with Jenson, aren't you?"

"I'm afraid not."

"Oh. I'm afraid I've been mistaken."

"You don't have to leave," Rush told her. "As a matter of fact, I wish you wouldn't."

The waiter was there, and she hesitated, then sat back down again. "Gin and tonic, please. Actually, I'm Mrs. Stanley P. Evans, and I guess I just assumed a man here by himself would be on business, and the rest of this week, business means Jenson."

"That sounds like a slogan," Rush observed.

"My God, don't tell my husband. He'll write it down."

Rush decided he liked her. "What does your husband do with Jenson?"

"He's a member of the board."

"He should be popular right now."

Judith Evans tilted her head. "Why?"

"I understand the sales and management people are here, too. It beats the usual downtown hotel convention."

"It's a special occasion."

"Oh?"

She gestured. "Some new process. I really don't know anything about it, but Stan and some of his colleagues are really all agog over it."

Rush did not pry. He suspected she was being truthful when she said she didn't know details. Clearly she was one of the loyal ones, a good company wife, ready to move where she was told, dress as she intuited was proper, be friendly with those who could be helpful, talk about things considered suitable. American industry owned a great many like her. They were often screened most carefully, along with their husbands. A wife who got too attached to a certain home, or insisted on choosing her own styles or friends, could gum up the works. It struck Milo Rush as a terrible way to live, or non-live. The amazing part was that so many not only accepted it but convinced themselves they were happy in the confines of the cookie-cutter. Judith Evans had come over and accosted him easily and with no sense of a problem because she had imagined he was One Of Us and so was to be treated in a friendly fashion. Given the description of a still sexually attractive woman who walked over and joined a strange man, and sat with him, a few curly pubic hairs peeping from the band of her swimsuit, because she liked his looks, and Judith Evans would have said the lady in question was a whore.

"Are you here with your family?" she asked now, cocking her head.

"No. I'm alone."

"What do you do?"

"Oh, I play a little golf, fly a plane, struggle with chess—"

She gestured impatiently. "I mean your *work*."

"Oh," Rush said, as if surprised. "I practice law."

Her eyes were sunny. "And are you a very good lawyer?"

"Of course."

"My husband plays golf. Maybe you'll get out together."

"That would be fine."

She was suddenly uneasy. "I'd better run along. It was nice meeting you, Mr. Rush." Since he did not work for the firm, she had run out of topics.

"Before you go," Rush said, "maybe you could tell me how long your meeting here will last."

"It starts formally in the morning. While the management level has its sessions, the board meets separately, of course. The dinner is Friday night, closing up."

"Two days."

"Yes."

"Are the Jenson people grouped in the lodge?"

"We have the two top floors, I understand. The fourth and fifth."

A movement toward the far end of the pool caught Rush's attention, and he turned his head. His was not the only head to turn. Walking up a pathway from the woods, Jane Clarken carried a towel and jar of suntan lotion. She was barefooted and her hair was loose. The black bikini was little more than two narrow straps, much briefer than the suit she had evidently used for sunning at home, because a narrow band of white showed between tan and bikini. The contrast made her look more nude.

"She's very beautiful, isn't she?" Judith Evans murmured.

"Yes, she is," Rush agreed.

They watched Jane walk to a vacant area at the far end of the pool, spread her towel, and sit down on it. She began applying lotion.

"Her name is Hendrix," Judith said.

"Oh?"

"Mrs. Walter Hendrix. I believe she's either widowed or divorced."

"Is that so?"

She turned quickly toward him. "You like her."

"As you said, she's very good-looking."

"I wouldn't have thought she was your type."

Rush smiled at her. "Really? What would you have said my type was?"

A touch of color not from the sun appeared in her cheeks. "It was just a stupid remark. Forgive me."

Rush offered her a cigarette.

She shook her head. "I really do have to run off now. It was nice meeting you, Mr. Rush."

"Possibly we'll talk again?"

She stood looking down at him with a younger woman's eyes in the loyal company-wife face. "Perhaps."

Rush thoughtfully watched her walk the length of the pool and into the hotel lobby. Then he turned slightly and peered again at Jane Clarken. Because of the distance she had not recognized him behind his tourist shades. She lay on her stomach now, sunning. Her face was toward him, but her eyes were closed. Rush felt an impulse simply to walk up to her and ask her what the hell was going on. He resisted.

Signaling the waiter, he signed the ticket for his tea and Judith

Evans's gin and tonic, then left the table to walk behind the cabana. He went down a sun-baked sidewalk beside the tennis courts and then onto a graveled path that led back into the trees.

The path took him on a meandering course into the woods. Most of the trees were pines, like living telephone poles that swayed in the imperceptible breeze in their tops, up where the sun was. Some few beech and maple and sumac struggled for survival at a lower level, and there was a dense brush of wild blackberries and raspberries, ferns, and ivy. It was much cooler in the woods.

He was almost on top of the first tree house before he saw it: a rounded, saucer-domed structure standing on brown-painted steel poles ingeniously placed among lower trees and brush, partially covered with ivy and painted a dull green to further blend in. The house seemed unoccupied, and he walked around it. An open redwood staircase curved up the side to a little porch. Windows looked out blackly from shuttered openings. There was a little graveled area to the side for a charcoal grill and a miniature clothesline rack. Nothing else of the natural setting had been disturbed.

Following the path, Rush found several other tree houses and discerned a pattern in their numbering: the pathway followed roughly a huge oval, and he was walking the numbering sequence backward from twenty-four.

Jane Clarken's house, number fourteen, had nothing to distinguish it from the others. Rush walked on around the oval and found himself on the edge of the fairway that led up to the green backing the swimming pool. There were no golfers in sight.

"Sir?"

"Yes," Rush said without turning.

"I wonder if I might speak with you a moment?"

"I was hoping you would, inasmuch as you've been following me since I left the tennis courts."

The man walked up behind Rush, and then came around in front to face him. He was quite young, with a squared-off face and black hair clustered in dense ringlets. He wore pale slacks and shirt. His eyes were troubled.

"I wasn't actually following you, sir. It just so happens—"

"What would you call it?" Rush asked, truly interested.

"My name is Barry Timmerman, sir." Timmerman reached into his hip pocket, took out a wallet, and handed over a card. "As you can see, I'm chief security officer for Jenson Company—"

"And I talked with Mrs. Evans." Milo Rush grinned.

Timmerman flushed. "No, sir."

"And Mrs. Evans talked back to me. *That's* it."

Timmerman's color heightened, but he was very young and determined. "No, sir."

Rush decided the boy was too serious to treat cruelly. "All right, then. What is it?"

"I thought we might just chat, sir."

Well, it was going to be difficult. "My name is Milo Rush, Barry. I'm a lawyer from Washington. Would you like to see some identification?"

"You have it all wrong, Mr. Rush."

"I'll give you my thinking and then you can correct me. You have a security assignment here for this meeting. That tells me there's something more or less secretive to be discussed, probably by the board of directors. All right. A lone man checks in coincidental with your own registrations. You see him talking to Mrs. Evans. You follow him and see him looking over the tree houses. You think, 'Maybe I'd better get some more information.' You could ask Mrs. Evans. You could check with the desk, perhaps. But you elect the direct approach, figuring no one would expect it. Now, where am I off base?"

Timmerman had listened intently, and now he smiled. "Only in a couple of minor details."

"The board meeting must look like a nasty one, if you're on edge."

"Oh, no. Nothing like that."

"But your instructions are to check out individuals who don't fit in well in a couples-family environment?"

"Actually—" Timmerman began, but then caught himself. His smile became a grin. "You're good at turning the questioning around, aren't you?"

Milo Rush shrugged. "Sometimes it works."

"I saw you check in," Timmerman added bluntly. "I already knew who you were, Mr. Rush, and it isn't difficult to check back credentials, even out here in the bush leagues. I followed you for a different reason."

"All right. What is it?"

"The security man for an outfit like Jenson sometimes does double duty for social arrangements. Mrs. Evans hopes you will have dinner with her and Mr. Evans tonight."

"The lady makes quick decisions."

Timmerman's color heightened slightly again, but he handled it well. "She has been known to do so, sir."

When Rush returned to the pool area, Jane Clarken had a companion. Sitting on a towel beside her and talking animatedly, the man was perhaps forty, nicely put together, with a rather old-fashioned short haircut that flattered his square-jawed features. He wore conventional blue swimming trunks, and had been swimming; beads of water gleamed on his arms, legs, and torso.

Not being able to afford the luxury of prolonged observation, Rush could only notice, walking past the cabana toward the lobby doors, that Jane seemed to be enjoying the conversation. Her head was tilted slightly to the side as she listened to something the man was telling her, and her smile was pleasant and attentive. For his part, the man was evidently going all out to be entertaining. It would have been very difficult for any man to be that close to Jane in her bikini and act otherwise.

Icy air conditioning closed around Rush as he entered the lobby. It crossed his mind to ask one of his newly found friends at the desk to identify Jane's companion, but the late-afternoon registration rush was well on, and a dozen couples stood around the registration desk with their luggage. Rush went up to his room and found the telephone ringing.

"Hey, bubba," Les Montgomery said over a scratchy connection, "I'm in town, still, and I thought I'd better check in. Some of our chickens are trying to come home to roost."

"What do you mean?"

"I called the office, per your instructions. Talked to Fred and then to Marty. She's had David Clarken on her ass all day. He's getting into a panic. He says if he doesn't have some definite word by six o'clock, he's just going to have to call the police."

"Christ," Rush groaned. "Did you give her the word I gave you?"

"I told her to tell him we've got his wife located, and she's all right, and not to worry. She said that was like saying the strontium 90 fallout really isn't bad until your skin starts falling off. She says he's been stewing in his own juice, and every hour you're gone, he gets that much more shook. She says we won't calm him down with any kind of message like I passed on."

Listening to his new headache, Rush closed his eyes and considered options. His first rush of irritation quickly vanished as he reflected on Dave Clarken's situation, knowing virtually nothing, out of touch, imagining the worst. Most husbands would react the same way. But calling the police now would only exacerbate the situation; there would be questions at the office as soon as Dave mentioned it, and then some telephone calls, and a visit from the local gendarmerie unless Marty played it very cool—in which case *she* would be hassled.

Rush put the problem on the other burner for a moment. "What did you find out about this outfit that's meeting here?"

Montgomery was profanely apologetic. Terrydale did not even have a public library. The local newspaper was a weekly, given over mainly to lead stories about three-pound bass. Jenson, headquartered in Cleveland, was bringing about two hundred people, counting wives and children, to Kenton's Run, and a gala time was going to be had by all. Jenson had recently been a feature in *The Wall Street Journal* for its diversification and growth, the local editor said. Did the local editor save *The Wall Street Journal*? No, he didn't have a subscription right now. He only got papers that would exchange, free.

"What do you want me to do?" Montgomery asked.

Rush decided. "Call Marty back. Have her get Dave to the office, or if it's past that time, have her take him to supper. Tell her to try to get a couple of drinks in him, calm him down if she can. Tell her to tell him Jane is all right, she's perfectly fine; I'm not only here, I'm with her, we're talking over some things, she's a little mixed up about some things, but there's nothing badly wrong, she loves him, et cetera. Tell her to tell him any damned thing she thinks will keep him calm, and away from the police, until you can get there."

"Till *I* can get there?"

"Get a rental car or a cab or a one-horse shay or whatever they have in that town and get back to Columbus. There ought to be some kind of early-evening commuter flight. Get to wherever Marty is holding Dave down. She can say you're flying back with a complete report, for that matter."

Montgomery sounded dubious. "What do I say when I get there?"

"Tell him more of the same. Make it out that Jane is having a little identity crisis and I'm with her and everything is perfectly fine."

"Is any of this true?"

Rush carried the telephone, on its long cord, to the closed draperies. He parted them slightly. He could see the poolside. Jane and her friend were at a canopy table, having drinks. She looked radiant.

"Enough of it is true," Rush said heavily, "to allow you to lay it on thick."

"What if he doesn't buy it?"

"Do your best, Les."

"But what if he still insists on the police?"

"Then let him go. Did you think I would tell you to knock him over the head or something?"

"If it goes that far, and the cops want to know where and who and how and why, do we cooperate?"

"Les, Dave may be upset, but he isn't a maniac. I think you can reassure him. He might not like it, but you can handle it. If all else fails, get on the horn and call me back from there, without letting him know where you're dialing. I'll try to deal with him myself."

"Okay, bubba. I think it's crap, but okay. Anything else?"

"I'll call you tomorrow at the office at straight-up noon."

"Look, if there's a hassle, *I'll* be calling *you* before then."

"Les," Rush said patiently, "I'm assuming there will be no hassle because you will handle everything beautifully. My call will be for the information."

"Information?"

"Les, our office *does* receive *The Wall Street Journal*. We *do* save the copies for a while. You *can* look up that article on Jenson."

"Oh!" Montgomery said. "Right! I see! I can dig it!"

"Get going," Rush ordered.

"You gonna be all right there by yourself?"

"I'll try."

"Hubba hubba!" And Montgomery broke the connection.

Five

GOING to dinner with the Evanses was a risk. Milo Rush considered the chances excellent that it would result in Jane Clarken's spotting him. But he could not hide in his room or behind big sunglasses if he was to penetrate what was going on here. He thought it would be interesting to see Jane's reactions if—as was likely—they were in the same room tonight. Beyond that he had some other plans.

When he went down to the lobby at 7:30, signs of the Jenson meeting had sprouted. There was a large easel near the reception desk announcing location of sales and management sessions, a luncheon, the board meetings, afternoon free time, and a cocktail dance Thursday night; more sessions were scheduled for Friday morning, along with a press conference at 2 P.M. Rush wondered what the conference was for. A banquet Friday night would close the two-day conference.

Walking past a registration table set up for Jenson arrivals, Rush started for the dining room. Vacationers, some well-dressed and some scruffy in shorts and thongs, milled around. Most of the children had vanished, perhaps to the tree houses with their parents. Through the glass windows overlooking the patio and pool area, Rush saw gas torches burning, tables, and a small combo on a corner platform. The musicians were wearing loud shirts and straw hats. The faint music sounded ersatz Hawaiian.

Judith Evans was standing near the entry to the dining room with a considerably older man. His severe dark suit and narrow tie contrasted sharply with her discreetly low pink cocktail dress. She had put her hair up and she looked very nice. Another couple stood by.

"There you are!" She smiled, extending her hand. "This is my husband, and this is Joe and Sally Gurney. Milo Rush."

Rush shook hands with Evans, getting a fleeting impression of tired, milky eyes and a soft hand. The man was startlingly older than his wife and gave off an aura of poor health. The Gurneys seemed more typical corporate people, he heavy-set, bluff and red-faced, she painfully slender, with a hectic, brittle quality.

"I understand you're here for a few days' rest," Evans said in a soft Texas drawl. His smile was low-key, as if he were resigned to something.

"Yes," Rush told him. "But for you people it's work, I hear."

Evans held the set smile. "I reckon we'll play a little." The smile, the tiredness of the eyes and the slump of his body bespoke enormous strains over a very long period, the kind from which a man could never wholly recover. But Rush detected a steely underside of the man that had not yet been weakened. Still a man to watch out for in a tight business transaction.

"Are you *the* Milo Rush?" Sally Gurney asked briskly. She wore a bright red sheath, and shouldn't have; it emphasized what time had done to her. Her eye makeup was too heavy and her hair too blue, in a tightly teased beehive that would have felt like fine wires to the fingertips.

"I recognize him from his pitchers, hon," Joe Gurney said before Rush could answer. "We got a celebrity in our midst."

Judith lightly touched Rush's arm. "They're having a luau on the patio. We thought that would be fun."

The hotel had done its best on atmosphere. Although pink and blue floodlights mounted high in the white face of the building bathed the area in soft light, and the sun still glowed behind dense cumulus clouds to the west, the gas torches flamed and smoked brightly. One corner of the pool had been roped off and plastic orchids floated. All the canopy tables had been arranged in a semicircle around a small dance area in front of the Hawaiian band, and tufts of dried grass had been tied to the canopies. The waiters wore shorts and loud shirts, and the waitresses, in bright muumuus, were barefooted. Rush saw that Lora, the younger desk clerk, had been pressed into service along with two blacks behind a portable bar. A long, low table along one side was laden with huge salads and other dishes heavily garnished with palm leaves and cut flowers. The combo—drummer, bass player, piano player, and guitarist doubling on a ukelele—was playing "Blue Hawaii." They looked bored.

"Isn't this *nice!*" Sally Gurney beamed as they sat down at a table halfway around the circle. "Look! There are the Pattons! Yoo-hoo! Hello! Isn't this nice?"

Rush had Judith Evans on his left and Joe Gurney on his right. Stanley Evans sat across the circular table beside Sally Gurney. Evans slumped in his chair, his smile still in place as he surveyed the scene with milky eyes.

"They've done a very nice job with this," he observed.

"I suppose they set it up in Jenson's honor?" Rush said.

"Well. Only about half our folks have gotten here so far. But we did let the management know we'd appreciate something a little extra."

Magically, the character of the crowd had changed since the afternoon. Although no one at his table had one, many of the others around the patio wore small name tags pinned to their lapels. Walking across the patio, Rush had seen one of the tags close-up. *Hello!*, they said; *I'm with Jenson, too! My name is*——. Jenson ran a tight ship.

A smiling waiter came by with little card menus for drinks. They featured things like The Lava Bowl, Pink Tahiti, and Waikiki Delight. Sally Gurney was ecstatic.

"You been here before, Milo?" Joe Gurney asked gruffly.

"First time," Rush said.

"By golly, it is for us too. But this is really a super place. You picked us a dandy place, Mr. E.!"

Evans languidly produced a cigarette and lighted it. "I believe in going out in style, Joe. What y'all do in future years is up to you."

"Stan is retiring with this board meeting," Sally Gurney explained. She reached over and patted Evans's arm. "And we are going to *miss* you, you sweet thing!"

"You're chairman of the board?" Rush asked.

"Past chairman. I've already stepped down from that, y' know."

"Jenson has grown fast."

Evans took a shallow breath. "That's all just about behind me now." He looked into the distance.

The waiter brought their drinks: scotch for Rush, VO and water for Evans, a frosty Cuba Libre for Judith, and a tall Pink Tahiti, with mountains of cherries and pineapple slices, for Sally Gurney. Her husband had ordered something called an Eruption; it was in a stoneware mug and had dry ice packed around the greenery so that it steamed lustily.

"Isn't this *fun?* Isn't this *nice?*"

Rush saw Barry Timmerman standing alone near the lobby doors. He wore a white dinner jacket with a carnation in the lapel. He was watchful. Jane had not shown up. Perhaps she wouldn't.

"I didn't realize, when we visited earlier today, that you were such a celebrity," Judith Evans told him.

"People tend to overstate things," Rush told her.

Her eyes were lively with admiration, and perhaps something more. "Yes. I would have expected you to say something like that."

"You try this little golf course?" Gurney asked.

"Not yet, no."

"Well, listen. You ought to. It's not half bad. You do play?"

"A little."

"Well, listen. Maybe Saturday, if you're still around, we'll get us a cart and go around a couple times. You still gonna be here then?"

"I may be. I haven't decided yet."

"Well, I sure won't have time before then. Big doin's tomorrow and Friday! But Saturday, that'd be real nice. Get us up a foursome."

Rush tried to draw Evans back into the conversation. "You play, sir?"

Evans gestured weakly. "I've given it up."

"You could start again, darling," Judith said.

"I'm too old, dear," Evans said quietly.

Judith cocked her head. "Did you ever hear of such a thing, Milo?"

Evans smiled again. "One must learn to accept his, or her, age."

Judith looked at her husband for an instant, and there was a glint of combined pain and anger. She quickly turned back to Rush. "I'll let you be the judge—"

"Never a judge." Rush smiled, trying to head it off. "I'm strictly the lawyer."

Sally Gurney giggled, but Judith would not be stopped. "If a man elects to retire at sixty-one, that doesn't mean his life is over, does it? Give us your frank opinion."

"Judith," Evans murmured.

Even Gurney seemed a little embarrassed. "Say! This is some drink! You know, I think it must have both rum and bourbon in it. I never tasted anything like it! You want to try it, Milo?" He offered the straw.

The band played "A Little Grass Shack in Hawaii." Heat steamed off the patio, making the first drinks go rapidly. Sally Gurney babbled about horseback riding tomorrow. Her husband leaned back, a slightly glazed look coming into his eyes as the Eruption proved its potency. The waiter came back and they ordered refills. More people filtered onto the patio, and some were now going through the food line. It was sunset. Rush spotted the man who had been nasty to the girls at the reception desk; his "wife" was about twenty years younger, with large features and flaming red hair worn long and loose, so that she looked like a stripper. Voices grew louder, making a constant background noise that often all but shut off the combo's music. A middle-aged couple, the man wearing a T shirt, shorts, and thonged sandals, the woman a shapeless yellow sun dress, moved into the center area and began dancing. They were a little crocked and having a good time. They backed apart and he started doing a corpulent hula. She began swinging her hips. A few people nearby grinned and clapped their hands.

"That's *awful*," Sally Gurney said surprisingly.

"She's just having a good time," Gurney said.

"She just looks vulgar. She doesn't look nice at all. That's not even a hula."

Judith said, "She's *trying* to do the hula."

"Well, it's just vulgar." Sally looked to Rush for corroboration.

"It's too bad," Rush said, "how often something looks vulgar just because it isn't very well done."

Judith looked at him and her eyes changed. "I would have expected you to say something like that, too." Under the table, her fingertips pressed against his thigh.

"At least," Sally Gurney huffed, "she isn't a Jenson person. She *isn't* one of us, is she, Stan?"

Evans seemed to summon considerable energy to turn in his chair. He studied the couple a moment, then turned back to his overflowing ashtray. "No. They're not ours."

"Any of the press contacted us yet, Mr. E.?" Gurney asked.

"No. Fortunately."

"Been no leaks, then, huh?"

"No. No leaks."

Judith said, "I think we're being rude to Milo, darling, talking in such a secretive way."

Evans gave her his set smile. "I'm sure Mr. Rush is aware generally of what we're discussing, dear. The *Journal* article's speculation was close enough that we aren't exactly sitting on a state secret, y'know."

"I missed the article," Rush admitted.

Gurney lighted a cigar. "Well, I'll tell you this much, Milo. Just don't buy a new car this year or next."

"You have a new engine development," Rush guessed.

Gurney winked at him. "Everything is confidential, right? We give nobody a hint on anything, right? Just don't buy a new car for a while, that's all."

"I'm sure Mr. Rush is discreet, Joe," Evans said slowly. "And engineering details and processing are really all we're holding. We'll surely make a general announcement, to open up certain negotiations, on Friday anyhow." He turned to Rush. "If you're interested in such matters."

"I'm fascinated." Rush smiled. "I assume you're talking about an engine development that ties into the emission control situation. I happen to be driving a new Oldsmobile with so much antipollution plumbing on it that you could mix milk shakes on the hood when the engine is at idle."

Evans's smile broadened slightly, and for the first time there was a real light behind his eyes. "Help may be on the way."

"Jenson is planning to move into the automotive engine field, then?"

"Jenson's recent corporate growth has been based largely on research and development. We aren't likely to go to GM or Chrysler or Ford and say, in effect, 'Y'all stand back and we'll manufacture your engines.' The production capacity is beyond our—or anyone else's—ability."

Gurney said, "We can sure sell ideas, though."

Evans nodded. "It's no secret, Mr. Rush, that a number of firms have been working very hard on new engine systems. As everyone knows, the internal combustion engine is probably doomed in its present form. Your new Oldsmobile is a case in point. Fuel leaning, retarded ignition timing, and recombustion of pollutants can be carried only so far, and then the engine simply does not perform. Frankly, the rotary engine will not be a long-term solution, regardless of what anyone says; it uses too much fuel, and fuel is becoming increasingly critical."

"I've heard of a Japanese system," Rush observed.

"There are at least two Japanese systems," Evans agreed. "One is very simple and works reasonably well on small engines if timing is kept perfect. The more complex system, as you probably know, in effect uses two combustion chambers, a small one where a rich mixture is ignited in the conventional way, and a larger one where the explosion of the rich mixture is sufficient to ignite an extremely lean one. It's a good compromise on the basic engine configuration."

"Which system is Jenson developing?" Rush asked.

Evans leaned back. "Something quite different."

Rush carefully grinned. "I'm still fascinated."

"I'm sure you are. A great many people are. In another six months to a year, I feel reasonably confident your answers will be forthcoming."

Rush nodded, turned to Judith, and changed the subject. He had learned more than he had expected to learn, and now some other things were beginning to make sense. He knew there was no way to cajole or trick Evans into giving another ounce of information. It had been a neat, harshly controlled performance, providing precisely what Evans wanted to provide and nothing more. Rush again revised upward his estimates on Evans. He wondered if it was the constant hard control that had made the man old before his time, or whether it was other factors.

In a little while it was dark around the pool area, and the torches were more dramatic, sending up crimson plumes. Most of the other hotel guests had retired to game rooms or to a small dance being held indoors, and, as if by signal, the Jenson people began filtering up to the luau table for food. Evans suggested joining them. Gurney said he wanted to wash his hands first. Rush joined him.

"Well," Gurney said loudly in the antiseptic glare of the restroom, "what do you think of Mr. E.?"

"He's quite a man," Rush said.

Gurney glanced around, making sure they were alone. "You better believe he's quite a man! Goddamn, what he's been through . . ."

Rush punched the machine that was supposed to dry hands but never did. The machine did as much as any of them ever did: it made a lot of noise.

Gurney talked louder, over the roar. "It's a good company. I've been with it for twenty years. I've got no complaints. But, by God, to see somebody like Mr. E.—well, it gets to you."

"He was forced out as chairman?" Rush said, guessing.

"I'm not telling tales out of school. I guess there're always two sides. But Mr. E. *built* this company. I guess it isn't all a bed of roses anywhere. But the way that man has changed in the last two years—it's enough to make you want to cry."

"Sometimes people get caught in changes," Rush said.

Gurney glared at him for an instant. "Yeah. And sometimes the best man gets screwed, too. . . . Come on. Let's go chow down. I'm hungry."

Whatever cross-currents were moving, the scene on the patio appeared pleasant and relaxed. The food was good enough, and everyone but Evans seemed to enjoy it. He picked at a few hors d'oeuvres and smoked endless cigarettes, smiling palely now and then as Sally Gurney told about last winter's trip to Europe. They had finished the meal, the dishes had been cleared, and the after-dinner drinks were being placed on the table when Rush saw Jane Clarken come out of the lobby.

He saw her instantly because he had been watching all evening.

She was wearing a silver dress, very simple and almost severe in its lines, with a shallow scoop neckline. The short hemline revealed enough of her lovely legs. Her escort was the same curly-haired man.

"Oh, look," Judith Evans said softly. "There's your girl."

Sally Gurney turned. "Whose girl? Where?"

"Milo's girl," Judith said.

"Oh, she's *lovely*, Milo! Who is she?"

"I have no idea," Rush said.

"But Judith said—"

"Judith is making a joke, I think."

Sally made a face. "Judith?"

"Milo has been admiring her from afar."

"Can't say I blame him," Gurney muttered.

Sally Gurney watched the couple move to a table on the far side. "It didn't," she observed with a trace of acid, "take Jack long to move in."

Gurney chuckled. "Nobody ever accused Jack of being slow."

"Jack," Judith Evans told Rush, "is our chief of development. Jack Moradian. And it does look like he's beating your time, Milo."

Despite himself, Rush felt a strong pang of irritation. He said nothing.

"Because," Judith added, "you do have the strangest way of looking at her."

Evans roused himself. As the evening had gone along, he had seemed to slump more and more, his mouth sagging and his eyelids hooding the pupils. "You suddenly seem intent on baiting our guest, Judith."

Across the room, Jane had been sweeping the area with her cool eyes. Now her gaze found Rush. It started to move on, then came back quickly. Her hand went to her throat.

"Did you see that?" Judith said. "You *do* know each other!"

Rush forced a smile. "How you carry on," he said softly.

"Does anyone know anything about the girl?" Sally Gurney asked.

"Her name is Hendrix," Judith said evenly, still watching Rush. "She recently lost her husband. Six months ago, it was. He was a banker in New York. She arrived yesterday from Washington. She's to be here a week. She's traveling alone."

"Well," Gurney grunted, "she isn't alone now."

Sally Gurney sighed. "Wouldn't you know Jack would find her *instantly?*"

Evans put another cigarette into the tray and immediately lighted a fresh one. "Jack is all right, Sally. He can be depended on."

"Can he?"

"Oh, yes."

"Well—I *hope* so!"

Gurney rubbed his thick hands over his protruding belly. "I think I'm going to have me some more of that purple sherbert." He made it rhyme with Herbert. "Anyone else want some more of that purple sherbert?"

It was a very bad shock for Jane Clarken.

She felt flushed, then cold all over. Immediately she knew she had to hide it. Somehow or other she managed. Jack Moradian was in the middle of saying something about a visit to Hawaii and didn't notice.

Milo's being here meant only one possible thing. He had followed her. It was the last thing she needed right now. She was already on a very fine edge, getting along only by sheer force of will. But Milo's being here could ruin everything. Anything could happen with him on the scene.

". . . but that was before the surfing." Jack Moradian grinned at her.

"It sounds like such fun!" She smiled.

"Not half so much fun as when we . . ."

She nodded, but her mind was not on his words.

She could not, she knew, allow Milo to remain here. He would see through everything, and then nothing would go right;

it would be ruined and then Joe Graeber would send the photograph copies to Dave, to newspapers—along with all the other evidence—and her marriage would be wrecked. She would stand a very good chance of going to jail. She couldn't let that happen. She was committed now and had to see it through. It was only another two days. She could handle it. But she had to get Milo to go away.

How? Telling Graeber was out of the question. There was no way to predict what he might do. She had to handle this herself.

Moving her eyes slightly, she could look past Jack Moradian's smile to the table near the lobby doors, where the man named Collins was seated alone. Collins's eyes flicked over her and moved on. He was watching every move she made.

But she had to do something. Now. Tonight.

At ten o'clock the band broke up, the platform was moved away, and some of the waiters began quietly dismantling the luau table. Part of the crowd had drifted off. The overhead floodlights had been shut off, and in the steamy night the only illumination was from the torches. The guitar player from the band came back and began performing solo on a Spanish instrument, his fingers moving smoothly over the wide fret board. He was very good.

"Isn't this nice?" Sally Gurney sighed. "So peaceful!"

Evans stifled a yawn. "Peaceful enough for this old man to be toddling off."

"It's early yet, Mr. E.!"

Evans smiled the same smile. "I find I need more sleep these days, Joe. We meet at ten tomorrow morning, you know, and while that might not seem early to some folks, it's going to be early enough for me."

Gurney grinned. "Want to be at your best, right, Mr. E.?"

"Yes, Joe. I want to be at my best."

Sally said, "It's been really nice, Mr. E., and I think you're a jewel for planning it."

"Well, Sally, the hotel really did that. We just dropped a suggestion."

She patted his hand. "You're still just a jewel. Just a *jewel*."

Evans looked toward his wife. "Judith?"

"I think I'll stay up just a while yet, dear."

Evans collected his cigarettes and lighter. "As you wish." He stood, somewhat bent over. "Mr. Rush. It's been a pleasure. I trust we'll see you tomorrow."

Rush shook the lifeless hand. "I'll be here."

Evans nodded to each of them. Suddenly he looked much older. "Good night, then."

They watched him walk into the hotel.

"Well," Gurney said explosively. "I don't know about you folks, but I'm going to have another drink."

"We ought to turn in soon ourselves, dear."

"Turn in? It's early yet!"

"You know how long it takes you to get started in the morning."

"I want to talk to Milo, here, about some of his famous cases."

"They're pretty dull in the telling," Rush told him.

"Milo is too modest," Judith said.

"Has he already told you?" Sally said. "Oh, dear! Then we'll never hear about them!"

"I think he'd rather talk about his girl, and where she's gone off to."

Sally made a face. "Back on that? You have a fixation, Judith!"

"I couldn't have put it better myself," Rush observed.

Gurney signaled the waiter, who came over trailed by a bellhop. The bellhop walked directly to Rush. "Sir? You have a telephone call on the lobby phone."

"She can't have gone far," Sally said. "Jack is still there, waiting for her."

Rush excused himself and followed the boy into the lobby. He was preoccupied with Judith Evans's insistence on talking about Jane, but he expected the call to be from Washington. He was surprised when he picked up the white telephone in the cubicle off the restaurant.

"Milo?" she said tautly.

"Speak of the devil," Rush said.

"I'm in my room and I have only a moment."

"What do you want, Jane? Or should I call you Mrs. Hendrix?"

"What do *you* want, Milo? What are you doing here?"

"It should be obvious."

"Milo, you have to leave this place right now."

"Why?"

"I don't have time to explain—"

"Or inclination either, I imagine."

"Milo, *please*."

"Do you want to meet me later and tell me what's going on here?"

"I can't."

"Do you want to tell me now?"

"I *can't*."

"Then get used to my company. I'm staying right here. I find myself devoured by curiosity about why a woman would leave her husband a lying note, buy a new wardrobe, and appear under an alias at a place like Kenton's Run."

"Milo." She sounded near tears.

He imagined her in her room. Other memories flooded back, and along with the bitterness in his throat was a sour ball of regret. "Sorry, babe," he said.

"You don't know what you're getting *into* here. If you'll just go away, I'll be back home late Saturday. I can promise you that."

"That's very sweet of you. I'm sure Dave will be delighted. Do you plan to bring Jack Moradian back with you, or is he the one you're really after?"

She drew in her breath audibly, and there was a pause. Then: "If you stay here now, there could be all kinds of trouble. I mean *serious* trouble, Milo. I can work this all out if you'll just leave me alone. Please, *please* go back to wherever you came from and stay out of it!"

"Sorry."

"Won't you—"

"Do you want to talk, now that you know I'm staying anyway?"

"You have to leave! You don't know what you're letting *both* of us in for if you stay."

"Sorry, babe," Rush said for the second time.

"Milo—!"

He broke the connection.

Back on the patio the crowd was thinner. The guitar player continued working, but he had stopped playing songs and was chording almost at random, making romantic flamenco sounds. They had ordered another round of drinks, including one for Rush.

"Hello again," Judith said huskily as he sat down beside her.

"Sorry about the interruption."

"A business call?"

"Of course."

"I was just saying," Gurney told him, "that I was a blamed fool for not bringing my fishing gear. Some of the boys have already hauled some nice bass out of that lake down there."

"The hotel must stock it," Rush said.

"Boy, I'd like to unstock it! Are you a fisherman?"

"I never got interested."

Gurney turned, craning his neck. Well beyond the pool, with the black vacancy of the golf course fairway in between, two small white lights shone on the surface of the water. "Somebody's night fishing down there now."

Sally Gurney sighed. "It looks romantic."

"It looks like fish for breakfast, kiddo!"

"I know what," Sally said, brightening. "Why don't the four of us walk down there!"

"What for?" Gurney asked.

"Well, we can stroll along the fairway, and go to the water's edge, and maybe take off our shoes and put our tocsies in. Wouldn't that be *fun?*"

Gurney sighed heavily.

"Oh, come on!" Sally insisted. "Let's!"

"Well, I suppose we can walk down there." Gurney was disgusted.

"Goodie!" Sally got to her feet a trifle unsteadily. "Come on, you two!"

"We'll stay here, Sally." Judith smiled. "You two run along."

"Oh, come *on!* It'll be *nice!*"

"I'm tired, dear. I'll probably toddle off to join my husband in a few minutes. Mr. Rush can keep me company until I finish my drink."

Sally made a rueful face. "If you want to come down after, Milo, we'll be along near where the lights are. All right?"

"Fine," Rush told her.

"Come on, Joey," Sally said, tugging Gurney's arm. "You can bring your drink along."

Gurney sighed again. "Guess we'll see you later, folks." He got up.

"If you change your mind," Sally told them, "just come on."

"Good night," Judith said.

Sally giggled. "Don't do anything we wouldn't do!"

Rush allowed himself a cigarette as he watched the couple move unsteadily around the pool and into the dark beyond.

Judith said, "I hope they don't both fall in."

"I didn't realize Sally was so far along until she started talking baby talk."

"Sally is a dear. But she does have a tendency to forget her limits."

They sat quiet for a while, listening to the guitarist. There were only about a dozen people left on the patio now; couples. The gas torches had been dimmed, the air had cooled. Quite suddenly it was that time of night when the party has wound down and those who remain are very much alone with one another.

The door of the lobby winked open.

"There she is," Judith murmured.

"Who?"

"Your girl."

"I told you, I don't even know her."

"I know you told me that, Milo."

Rush said nothing, watching in the dimness as Jane went back and rejoined Jack Moradian.

Judith said, "Did I make you very angry, insisting she was your girl?"

"It's not the kind of verbal game I enjoy."

"Then I'm sorry."

"Let's forget it."

67

"Of course you know I'm jealous."

Rush looked at her, and her eyes were very open with it.

"I'm forty-five," she said huskily. "I'm really not too old, am I?"

"Judith, meeting you has been the nicest thing that's happened to me here. But—"

"I'm Stan's second wife," she cut in. "I was his secretary. I took him from his first wife. He was my age now when we were married. People told me the difference in our ages would matter, but it didn't matter. Not for a long time."

Milo Rush did not want this to go on. He liked her. He felt a faintly bitter sense of inevitability. He could not stop her from going on.

"I've been a very good wife," she told him calmly. "Stan loves his work. He always gave everything to his work first. I didn't complain. I moved where Jenson said we should move, dressed the way Jenson said I should dress. When he became a member of the board, I even changed churches . . . to one more fashionable.

"It's only in the last two years that he's become the way you saw him. I don't know exactly what happened, and I never will. We don't—talk about things that matter. He's an old man now. He shouldn't be, but something broke him."

"Judith—"

"But I'm not old," she went on. "And I'm not broken. I think you're alive just as long as you're trying things—or just *trying*. They can't beat me, not ever. Because I won't quit."

She paused, watching him. He did not know what to say.

"So you really like me?" she asked abruptly, as if it mattered.

He smiled at her. "Yes. I think a lot of people must really like you."

"I like you, Milo Rush. More than anyone I've met in a very long time."

He hesitated, trying to choose his words properly, because he did not want to hurt her in any way.

She said, "Will you please take me upstairs now?"

"All right."

She stood. "I'll wait for you by the elevator."

Rush signaled the waiter and signed the ticket. He put out his cigarette in the ashtray and glanced around. Jane was still there in the shadows with Moradian. They were sitting close together, but discreetly so. Rush took a deep breath and walked across the patio area to the brightly lighted lobby, his hand in his pocket closing on his room key. He was not at all sure what he was going to do.

He went into the lobby and walked toward the elevators. Two other couples stood there, and Judith. Her eyes were at pinpoints from the bright light, and she looked very pale and very vulnerable. Wisps of her hair had fallen down. In the bright light she looked like a housewife who had wandered, after a party, into the corner deli for a loaf of bread.

"There you are," she said, smiling. As the elevator door slid open, she tried to slip her hand into his.

They got into the elevator with the other two couples, who were talking softly. One of the men punched a button. "What floor, folks?"

Rush turned to her. "What floor is your room, Mrs. Evans?"

She blinked, the only sign of the blow. "Six."

The others got off on three. The ride on up to six was in silence. The elevator door hissed open.

"Good night," she said huskily.

"I'll walk you to your door," he said.

She looked back at him as she pressed the button to close the elevator door before he could get off. "No." The door closed.

Rush rode back down to his floor. It was very quiet in the elevator, alone.

Six

WITH the draperies drawn tightly across the windows of the state park cabin, Joe Graeber was methodically checking out his electronic gear and cameras when he heard car tires on the gravel. He peered out, gun in hand, then relaxed and put the automatic back in the hip pocket of his coveralls. He went to the door of the one-room cabin and swung it open long enough to let Schmidt enter. He then closed the door again, shooting the bolt.

"You're prompt," Graeber told Schmidt, glancing at his chronograph. "I said nine Thursday morning, and you're here at nine Thursday morning. Good. You can see I've got the equipment in. Now—"

"Joe," Schmidt interrupted, "we've got a problem."

His stomach tightening, Graeber looked more closely at Schmidt's thin face. "The bitch ran out."

Schmidt grimaced. "No, nothing like that."

"What, then?" Graeber snapped. "Our man is there, isn't he? When I talked to her yesterday, she said that was affirmative."

The cabin was utilitarian—a tiny kitchen corner, pine bunk beds, a hideaway sofa, chairs and table. Schmidt dropped onto the couch and nervously ran his hands through his hair. "Somebody else is there. He's aware of our girl's real identity."

"How did you find out?" Graeber asked, his fists balling. "Goddamn it, if that miserable whore told somebody—"

"Calm down, calm down. It's not like that at all. She handled it all right. She's doing everything right. The only way we picked this up was that bug you had us put on the phone in her room."

Graeber's anger seethed. "She did call somebody, then?"

"No. He forced her. We picked it up on the tape. He appeared, she recognized him and tried to run him off."

"Have you got the tape?"

Schmidt removed a small envelope from his pants pocket. "We dubbed it over on a cassette. We wanted to have the full spool in case there was more to come."

Graeber strode to the kitchen table and shoved off the rolls of light, Alpine-type climbing rope and the magnesium alloy grappling hooks. He pulled a cassette recorder into the vacated space, flicked it open, and took the cassette from Schmidt. "When did this happen?"

"Last night."

Graeber snapped the cassette into place and turned the machine on.

"*Milo?*" the machine rasped. Graeber stiffened as he recognized Jane Clarken's voice.

"*Speak of the devil,*" a man's voice said.

"*I'm in my room and I have only a moment.*"

"*What do you want, Jane? Or should I call you Mrs. Hendrix?*"

Schmidt said, "See? He knows—"

"Shut up. Shut up. Lemme hear this."

His ulcer sending out stabs of pain, Graeber listened to the remainder of the conversation. When the voices stopped and the recording was finished, he stood there long moments, listening to the hiss of blank tape.

Finally he reached out and stabbed the "off" button on the machine. "Who is he?"

"Milo Rush," Schmidt said. "He's a Washington lawyer. Maybe you know who he is—"

"That's affirmative," Graeber broke in. "God almighty! How did *he* get in on this?"

"He's a friend of hers and her husband."

Graeber kicked the coils of rope against the cabinet doors. "Just what we needed! Everything going A-okay, and something like this pops up!"

"She didn't see him," Schmidt said. "There's been no more contact."

"What did you do about him?"

"We haven't done anything about him."

"You didn't take him out?"

Schmidt's eyes widened and his goiter worked. "Take him out?"

"Take him out! Take him out! You don't understand English anymore?"

"My God, Joe, this is a prominent man. If anything happened to him, we'd have law from every place down on us!"

"It didn't ever occur to you, maybe, to get him to your room and lock him up? Just put him out of action until you could check with me?"

"He's made some new friends at the lodge, Joe! They'd be looking for him. And you can't just . . . we couldn't just . . ." Schmidt's mouth worked. "This isn't the Agency, Joe. You can't just—take people *out* like that."

Graeber picked up a water glass and hurled it into the sink. It was plastic, and instead of a satisfying crash, it bounced with a hollow *thunk!* It made him more furious.

"Did you ever think," he said, "that we've got almost a quarter of a million dollars at stake in this job? I don't care if it's the Agency or the Girl Scouts of America. For a quarter of a million dollars, if some son of a bitch's body has to float down the river—"

"Joe, wait a minute," Schmidt pleaded. "Listen, now. Calm down. If we have to, we can get him out of action long enough for this job tonight."

"It's just fourteen hours from now!"

"I *know* that. But we've got the masks anyway, haven't we? All right, then. We can cool him long enough. He can't recognize us. No harm done, Joe. Just calm down, okay?"

Graeber bit at the stub of a fingernail, making it bleed. He spat the shred of cuticle. Sometimes he had difficulty remembering his situation. He had to remember he was on his own now. He couldn't count on anyone to send in new men if something went wrong . . . if he pushed somebody too far and they opted out. He had to have Schmidt, especially now. And he had to be careful. It was maddening to be careful. Boldness had always been his trademark. He should not be in this stinking state park cabin, hiding, having to deal with incompetents. It was unfair.

"How's she doing on her part?" he asked.

"The girl?"

"The girl, affirmative," Graeber said sarcastically.

"She's doing great. I been holed up, but Collins has been there all the time. He said Moradian made for her like a bee to honey."

"Tonight?"

"Collins says no sweat, he's sure to ask her."

"Has he asked her yet?"

"They just met, Joe."

"Goddamn. What's the matter with the son of a bitch? Does he think he's got all week to make her?"

"It's okay, Joe. Really."

Graeber closed up the recorder, passed an eraser over the cassette, and handed it back to Schmidt. "I'll be there at noon. You get back. Tell Collins to stay on her. You take over on this Rush character."

"Watch him?"

"Affirmative. When I get there at noon, I'll give you some words."

"Do you want me to take any of this gear back in my car?"

"Negative. I'll bring it. We'll move it in later."

Schmidt seemed to be relaxing. "You've got everything?"

"You better believe it."

"The other guys. When do they check in?"

This was bad news, but Graeber pretended unconcern. "There's only one."

"*One!* You said—"

"One's enough. He's already there. We'll huddle late this afternoon."

"But with just one other guy, Joe—"

"I said it's enough, didn't I?"

Schmidt looked like he wanted to argue. Graeber glared at him. Schmidt backed down. "Whatever you say. It's your plan."

"You better believe it," Graeber told him. "Now move it."

Schmidt obeyed. As he listened to the car drive away on the gravel road, Graeber thought about the two good men who had been stupid enough to get themselves busted in Miami right on the eve of the operation. He bit off another piece of cuticle. He would just have to make do, he thought. He could manage. He always had.

By midmorning, the opening of Jenson's meetings was very apparent at Kenton's Run. Nearly all the men had vanished behind closed doors. From the main auditorium at the west end of the ground floor, a recorded voice and music boomed through the walls. A sales film was in progress. On the lower level the board of directors had also begun a preliminary session. That area was quiet.

On the patio, Milo Rush stirred his black coffee by habit. It had been a year since he had given up sugar, but stirring the coffee remained a vaguely soothing operation. As always, a part of his mind ticked off pros and cons on the extra few hundred calories per day that better coffee would cost him. As always, he decided he could take it straight one more day, just as he could restrict himself to six cigarettes today, as opposed to the three packs he would smoke if he let go. It got awfully tiresome, controlling so many gross impulses. He figured that if he ever let go, he would be a three-hundred-pound blob of lung cancer within six months, but there still were days when the chance seemed almost worth taking.

He had been up early, watching some night fishermen come in and the first groups hit off the number-one tee. He didn't know exactly what he was looking for, but sleep had been impossible anyway; he felt edgy. The fact that one of the first golfers on the tee had spoken to him had turned out to be a bonus.

Wearing bright golf shorts and a net T shirt, the man came over with a tentative smile. He was of medium height, in his fifties, with modish sideburns that made it appear he was struggling a little too hard to seem younger.

"Mr. Rush," he said, extending his hand.

Rush shook hands with him.

"I'm Win Jenson, Mr. Rush. I heard you were registered. It's a pleasure."

"So there really is a Jenson with the company." Rush smiled.

Jenson swung his driver, practicing a compact backswing. "I hope to tell you there's a Jenson. I'm the fella himself. You know our company?"

"Only by general reputation."

"My father started with horse-drawn wagons. Now we're into a little bit of everything. I believe in growth as an antidote to old age."

It was a puffy statement, and Rush decided he might not like Mr. Win Jenson. On the tee box, the first of Jenson's partners hit, the second teed up his ball. Rush said nothing, although Jenson eyed him speculatively, as if expecting comment.

Jenson finally said, "I saw you last night with some of our people."

"Yes," Rush said.

"The Gurneys and the Evanses."

"That's right."

"Known them long?"

"No."

Jenson swung again, grunting. "Good people. Old Evans used to be quite a man. He's pretty well used up now, I'm afraid."

"I understand he's retiring soon."

Jenson frowned as he watched the second player hit. "Yep. I hope to tell you he is. This is his last meeting. It's one of those painful things in business, Mr. Rush, seeing a man wear out and have to be forced out."

"I wasn't aware he was being forced out."

"Well, I shouldn't have mentioned it. But then I think it's no big secret. Sometimes, with age, a man's judgment goes, Mr. Rush."

One of the men on the tee called, "Come on, Win."

Jenson frowned. "In a minute."

"We need to hit, Win. People waiting."

Jenson glanced at the half-dozen men standing back off the tee box, clubs in hand. Evidently he didn't see any familiar faces. "They can wait a minute." He turned back to Rush with a smile. "Care to join us for a quick nine holes?"

"Thanks, no."

"Possibly later. The wife and I might work you into our dinner plans."

"I wouldn't want you to put yourself out."

"No trouble, no trouble. I'll have Timmerman or someone check with you later, if you like."

"Come on, Win!" one of the players called pleadingly.

"Do you play tennis?" Jenson asked.

"A little," Rush said.

"I may look you up before supper, then. I'll have to warn you. I'm considered a very strong player."

"Probably out of my league, then."

"Try to play every day." Jenson swung the club again. "Nothing sadder than a man who gets old before his time."

"It might not be so much of a problem, though, as long as he owns the company."

Jenson looked up sharply. "How was that?"

"My little joke."

"Come on, Win! Please!"

Evidently they had said the magic word. Jenson turned. "Well. See you later, Mr. Rush." He went to the tee, took another practice swing, and hit the ball as Rush would have predicted: short and down the middle.

Now, sipping his acrid coffee under the hazy glare of a cloudy sky, Rush wondered idly what was happening in the board meeting room. For at least two reasons, it was an important series of meetings: Stanley P. Evans was stepping down formally —being forced out, if Jenson's boast had been accurate—and key decisions were being considered on the new engine development. It was clear that neither decision was cut and dried. Evans had friends and admirers, Gurney among them; Gurney was not the type of man who would step out and render an opinion if he was alone, so it was likely that Evans's demise was a very close thing. And the engine configuration, whatever it might be, was the type of project on which companies rose or fell. Behind the façade of a pleasant family outing, Jenson was in far-reaching turmoil.

Rush tried to imagine a way that Jane Clarken's presence, under an alias, might fit directly. He could see certain obvious potentialities with Jack Moradian, but he couldn't link up the various other factors he now understood.

He had been waiting to see Jane today. She had not yet appeared. He had managed to spot Moradian entering the morning board meeting. If Jane's recognition last night had been as much of a shock to her as it seemed, she had not been too panicked by it. Rush had expected some follow-up after her telephone call, but nothing had happened. He was left in the kind of position he did not particularly like: he could stand pat and wait until a discernible false move was made, or he could go to Barry Timmerman and blow the whistle on Jane. Neither option was very good.

Finishing his coffee, Rush leaned back and decided to deny himself cigarette number one for another hour. A number of company wives had gathered around the pool, some with children. He watched them. Although the women varied in age and appearance, from one rather young woman in a pretty one-piece swimsuit to several older women in almost somber summer dresses and hats, even a casual onlooker might have guessed they all belonged to the same company or organization. There was a cookie-cutter languid smile, a quiet withdrawal of resignation. *See us having fun,* they said; *see us being loyal.*

From the cabana area, Judith Evans walked out and joined the rest. She sat down with a small group of women who seemed middle-management, neither the oldest nor the youngest, with children. The others seemed to treat her nicely. It was important to be nice.

She spotted Rush and waved briefly in greeting. He waved back. She did not come over. He was thankful for that.

Jane Clarken inspected herself nervously in the mirror and left her tree house promptly at 11:30. She entered the lodge on the lower level and rode alone in the elevator, the air cool on her bare legs and arms. Her last glance in the bedroom mirror had shown her as really quite lovely, with everything in order, the white shorts and sleeveless jersey blouse immaculate against the bronze of her skin. She wore white sandals and carried a tiny straw purse. The soft blouse clung subtly to her breasts, and her nipples were sharply erect; she was not used to going without a bra, although she hardly needed one, so that even the movements of walking to the lodge had made her tips harden. If she moved just so, now, a person would be able to see that she was naked beneath the tennis costume.

There was a bitterness in her throat. She had imagined tricks like this were all behind her. How well she remembered and still used them. And that made her every bit a bitch.

As she left the elevator she spied Jack Moradian standing with a group of men in the lobby near the registration desk. The lobby was in hubbub as meetings evidently had just broken up. When Moradian saw her, he detached himself from the others and walked over, a hard-covered portfolio under his arm.

"Hi," he said, grinning. "Did you sleep well?"

"Well, and late." She smiled in response.

He looked her up and down with frank admiration. "You look great."

"And you look *very* businesslike."

"Hell. That's how I'm supposed to look today."

"And so severe!"

"If you were giving this presentation this afternoon and tomorrow, you'd be severe too. No, I take that back. You couldn't look severe if your life depended on it."

Jane stifled a little yawn, giving him a chance to notice. "Are we having breakfast?"

He grimaced. "I've got a damned luncheon in a half-hour."

"Oh, dear."

"I know it. Crap. They added it on. I can't get out of it."

"I understand, Jack."

"If you're going into the coffee shop, could I join you until I have to go on downstairs for the grim business at hand?"

She tilted her head at him. "I think that would be grand."

They walked through the crowd, heading for the tiny coffee shop in the east corner of the building. She was aware of the glances she got—some open, some covert, all (except for a few from other women) admiring. This was not unpleasant. The kind of job this was, despite her hatred of it and the backgrounding circumstances, had aroused old instincts. She was acutely aware of her body and every movement. She was a splendid animal and could not abstain from taking pleasure in it.

If she could just really and truly end it with this job, she thought, it might not be so bad. Dave need never know. She could somehow keep Milo Rush out of it and persuade him not to tell Dave. Then it would be all right and she would forget about it—someday. . . .

The coffee shop, which catered to the doughnuts and coffee trade, was quiet and deserted. Moradian led her to a corner table where, she noticed, they could not be seen from the lobby. He put his large portfolio case on the extra chair and signaled the waitress. Jane ordered coffee and toast.

"Is that the extra-special project?" she asked, indicating the portfolio case.

"That's it, locked and double-locked."

"Have you started yet?"

"No, sometime this afternoon. We're all locked up in reports and personnel matters."

"It sounds awful."

He glanced at his watch.

"You have to go now," she said regretfully.

"No, not for a while yet."

"I don't want you to be late, Jack. After all, we do have this evening."

He frowned nervously. "About this evening."

"Yes."

"Is that your answer?"

"Was *that* the question?"

"Jane, I don't want to make it sound like I'm trying to rush you along. But you know—well—we did have a nice time last night. I like you."

She looked into his earnest eyes and wondered why the sweetest ones were sometimes the ones who had to be hurt. "I like you too, Jack. Really. I think you already know that."

He looked down at the tablecloth while the waitress brought the coffee and toast. He did not look up when she went away. "I know you lost your husband . . . not too long ago," he said slowly. "The last damned thing in the world I want is to make anything between us seem cheap, like one of those ski lodge things."

She put her hand briefly over his. "I know."

"We had talked about going over toward Terrydale tonight, to that folk festival. Are you sold on doing that?"

"Why, Jack?"

"I thought we might stay around closer. We could have dinner here. There's going to be music on the patio again tonight. We might just . . . have a quiet evening here."

"That sounds lovely, Jack."

"You mean that?"

"Of course I do."

"You know. Dinner, dancing, and then a little later, possibly we could get off somewhere by ourselves."

She looked directly at him. Her pulse stirred. *You're going to be so sorry,* she thought.

He smiled. "Sound all right?"

"Yes," she said softly.

Having seen them enter the coffee shop, Milo Rush checked his watch. It was almost time for Les Montgomery's noon call from Washington. Rush found the elevator area jammed and used the stairs to go up to his floor. Les's call, he thought, was going to answer several questions. The fact that there had been no calls earlier indicated that he had managed to calm Dave down somewhat. But the newspaper clipping about Jenson might be very helpful.

He was still undecided about going to Barry Timmerman. That, he thought, would be a last-gasp decision, one he could still put off for a little while. Whatever precisely was in the wind, it was unlikely that anything would crystallize before nightfall.

Unlocking the door to his room, he stepped inside and closed it behind him. The maids had done their work, the bed was made, fresh linens were on the dresser, and the draperies had been restored to their closed position. The sun was bright gold behind the pale fabric.

Milo Rush reached for his first cigarette, concluding that he had the afternoon relatively free to check out the few angles remaining to him after the telephone call came in.

Which was absolutely wrong.

As he turned from the door of the room, there was a movement in the darkened bathroom.

A man stepped out to face him, then another. Rush first noticed their guns, and then the fact that they wore grotesque Halloween masks.

Seven

ONE of the masks was Goofy and the other was Frankenstein. Both guns were lightweight police specials. In his left hand Goofy had another item of police equipment, a blackjack.

"Even UNICEF doesn't trick or treat this early," Rush told them.

"Funny," Goofy said. "Turn around. Face the wall."

Knowing what was coming, Rush had to obey anyway. He had no sooner turned than the sap crashed into the left side of his head, toward the back, just where the manuals said to use it. The pain erupted like fire through the base of his brain, and then things darkened and turned around, and he vaguely felt himself hit the floor.

"Not too hard! Not too hard!" That was Frankenstein.

"I tapped him easy. Hurry up. He won't be out long."

Rush was not fully out at all, but the blow had dazed him, and he could not move as one of the men rolled him over on the floor, the shag carpet digging into his face, and pulled his arms behind his back. He felt something hard and cool on his wrists and couldn't get his arms around where they should be again. Something rubbed against his mouth.

"Before we move him or after?"

"Now. Hurry up."

They fiddled with his legs. He understood they were tying his ankles, tight. It hurt. Then they talked about something for a moment, and he could not make any sense of it whatsoever. He felt himself being lifted and was aware that he was so limp they were having a hell of a time with him. They were grunting and giving each other orders, moving him around a corner. Their voices echoed against hard surfaces, and it was dark. Then they swung him and set him down hard, with something cool and unyielding against his back. He opened his eyes and it was not dark at all, only dim, because lights were shining on the black tile of the bathroom. They had put him in the bathtub.

Frankenstein was bending over him, wrapping something lightweight and yellow around his arm. Tubing.

"The whole thing?"

"No. He probably gave us enough for a horse."

"Half?"

"Half is good."

Frankenstein had a hypodermic syringe in his hands. Rush distantly felt the needle bite into his arm. He could not get it all together to protest.

Something ruffled and rattled, and they had drawn the shower curtain across the tub area. Beyond the curtain it suddenly went black as the light was turned out. Rush heard the two men muttering to each other, and then a door closed softly. It was quiet except for the hiss of air conditioning and the drip of a faucet.

The telephone began to ring. It rang and rang. Rush listened to it for a while, but then a new darkness crept into his mind and he knew nothing.

In Washington, Les Montgomery frowned at Marty as he hung up the phone. "What do you know about that?"

"No answer?"

"The little girl on the switchboard there says nope."

"Maybe he went on to lunch."

Montgomery doubted it. "Or maybe I'm a little early. I'll wait a few minutes and give him another honk."

As the afternoon wore on, Judith Evans wondered increasingly about where Milo Rush had gone off to.

For a while after lunch she had told herself she didn't care one way or the other. Last night had hurt her. But secretly she knew, despite her pique, that he had treated her in the only way that would have left her anything at all this morning. She was not a cheap resort pickup. And he was clearly not a man who took any advantage. There had been no actual rejection, she realized now. He had handled it perfectly. They knew each other a little better now, and would be more wary. And if something happened tonight . . . or tomorrow night, it would not be a cheap mutual taking, as it would have been if he had taken her boozily to his room after the luau.

Even if nothing happened, they had faced a moment together, and there might be another time, another place. This was worth remembering, and it made her feel of genuine value, something she needed badly.

So she looked for Milo Rush after lunch, after she had begun to work these feelings out.

At first she lay by the pool, getting in to get wet now and then, and idly watched the lobby doors. He did not appear. When the sun began to be uncomfortably intense on her back and legs, she went upstairs to change, going through the cabana so she could look over the tennis courts. He was not there.

After a cool shower and a change into a light dress, she went downstairs again. The meetings droned on. Some of the wives had gone on a sightseeing tour, others were horseback riding, and a few were playing golf. Possibly others were in town or scattered around the grounds. Judith had turned down the bus ride to the Hocking Hills, and so was now at loose ends.

She idled through the game room, the souvenir shop and the big lounge, where a color TV set flickered before empty chairs. Going out past an alcove where some children were whacking pool balls around a coin-operated table, she walked in the dense afternoon humidity past the tennis courts again. One court was empty; on another two boys were playing, and on the third two couples were playing mixed doubles. She paused under the shade of a maple tree and watched the two men and women play a few points. They were having fun. She felt a stab of loneliness.

The gravel path led her past several of the tree houses and then down a slope that looked out from trees onto one of the golf course fairways, with the lake gleaming beyond. She saw some men walking up the fairway. One was tall, fair-haired, with a solid, slender build. For an instant her pulse moved faster. Then the man got close enough so that she could see he was not Milo Rush after all.

He was around somewhere, she thought. Her inquiry at the desk proved he had not checked out . . . had not left in order to dodge her completely. So he was here, somewhere, possibly horseback riding, although it did not seem like his style. It would be all right. He would show up.

Her eagerness to see him again was frighteningly intense.

"It was stupid, not getting a poolside room," Joe Graeber said.

Daugherty folded thick hands on his belly and looked around the bedroom. "I raised hell. Damned near got in a fight with some joker. Did no good."

Graeber shrugged. "You could have watched for the lights and would have known exactly when to move, that's all. This way we have to use the walkie-talkies."

"That's what you brought them for, wasn't it?"

"Naturally," Graeber lied. "It would just have been simpler if you had been able to get a room where you could just look out your window and watch the lights."

Daugherty grunted but didn't say anything.

"The girl you brought along as your wife," Graeber said. "Is she going to be any trouble?"

Daugherty grinned. "No way."

"You're sure you can keep her out of your hair?"

"Listen, the way she soaks up the juice, the only question is whether she passes out at nine or ten."

"Make it nine," Graeber suggested.

"Got you."

"And if she gives you any trouble, lower the boom on her."

"She won't give me any trouble, Joe. She's an old friend."

"Not too old," Graeber pointed out acidly.

"What do you mean by that?"

"I mean it would have been better to bring an older woman."

"Why?"

"Who's going to believe she's your wife?"

"Who has to believe it?"

85

"That's the way you registered."

"You think I'm the first guy ever checked in here with a young chick listed as his wife?"

Graeber sighed. "I suppose."

"Besides, she fucks like a mink."

"I'm not interested in that. Just as long as she doesn't mess anything up."

"She won't. Hell. She's stupid."

"As far as she knows, this is just a vacation?"

"Sure."

"Good. Because if anything goes wrong, you know what your story is."

"I know what my story is," Daugherty said, betraying concern for the first time, "but what could go wrong?"

"You could have a heart attack while you're in his room," Graeber said sarcastically.

"Okay, okay. If anything does happen, I know what I'm to say."

"And you *stick* to it. That's important. All they can possibly try to stick you with is burglary in the second, and with the story you'd tell, the chances of bringing charges ain't very big."

"I know," Daugherty said. "Only there won't be any slip-ups, so not to worry, right?"

Graeber glanced at the man. *If you only knew*, he thought. "Affirmative," he said briskly.

"Does that page go all over the hotel?" Les Montgomery asked.

"Yes, sir," the girl at Kenton's Run told him over the long-distance connection.

"Well, look: Is there anyplace else around there you might try?"

"Sir, I've tried the cabana, the bar and the pro shop. There just aren't any other telephones."

"You know Mr. Rush, do you?"

"I know him by sight, yes, sir."

"Have you seen him around there lately?"

"I saw him sometime this morning, sir."

"Not since?"

"No, sir."

Montgomery thought furiously. "Look, are you at the main desk?"

"I'm in the office right behind it, sir—"

"You can see the front parking lot, right?"

The girl sounded mystified. "There's a window, but—"

"Do me a favor," Montgomery pleaded. "Look out at the lot."

"Sir, I can't—"

"Right out in front," Montgomery insisted. "In the row that goes right out from the front, there. About four, five cars from your end, facing east, there ought to be a dark green Chevrolet. Do you see that?"

There was a pause and the sound of something being moved near the telephone. "Sir, there are so many cars—"

"Four or five from the end. Facing east. A dark green Chevrolet, two-door, white-walls—"

"There is a car like that parked fifth from the end, sir."

"Okay. You're a doll baby. Will you please try Mr. Rush's room just once more?"

"I've tried twice on this call, sir—"

"Humor me."

She sighed audibly and cut him into the circuit. This allowed him to hear her dialing, and the instrument in Milo Rush's room begin to ring. Montgomery listened to it ring repeatedly. His nerves had begun to tighten painfully.

Over the tenth ring, the girl asked, "Is that enough, sir?"

"Yes," Montgomery said. "Thanks."

Leaving his tiny office, he went down the carpeted corridor to Milo Rush's waiting room. Marty was there alone, typing.

"Any luck this time?" she asked.

"No. Listen. If Dave Clarken calls again, tell him I had to run some errands, right? Tell him everything is cool."

She wrinkled her forehead, looking doubtful. "I wasn't very successful yesterday."

"I think I've got him looking at it right. I think it ought to be okay."

"Where are *you* going?"

Les Montgomery paused in the doorway. "Hell. I'm starting to get dizzy. Back to Ohio again."

Clouds trundled out of the north late in the afternoon, releasing a steady drizzle that emptied the pool and chased everyone off the patio area. Judith Evans went to her room, irritably selected a magazine, switched on the floor lamp and began to read.

A little after four, she heard voices in the hallway outside and recognized her husband's among them. A key turned in the door and he entered.

"Oh," he said. "There you are."

"Here I am," she murmured, and by an effort of will managed to hide her reaction.

His appearance shocked her. Earlier she had hoped it would be one of his good days. He had seemed buoyed by the prospect of the meetings and was alert with nervous energy; he had gone to the morning session wearing a bright—for him—shirt and tie, and at lunch his color had been good and he had remained energetic in appearance.

Now it was as if his spirit had been punctured. His tie was askew and the collar wilted by perspiration. His thinning hair seemed pasted to his skull, which had assumed death-mask tightness over his face. His eyes were sunken, dazed. With slumping shoulders he seemed to close the door behind him only by dint of enormous effort. He moved to the bed like a zombie and stretched out on it without removing his shoes, an act very unlike her meticulous husband.

"Was it a hard meeting?" she asked, as if not too concerned.

"Oh," he said wearily, and did not continue.

"Did you present your final resignation?"

He stared at the ceiling. "Yes."

"And was it . . . accepted?"

"Yes."

So that hope, too, had gone. She knew he had imagined they might somehow have a change of heart and urge him to stay on. She had watched him build this futile hope, like other futile hopes before it, and in seeing her man grasp at such straws she had felt things inside her die. There was nothing now she could say.

He sat up as if unable even now to deny the kinetic energies that had driven him. He was very pale. "Jack Moradian outlined the engine proposals, where we stand and where we're going. He explained how close we are on everything but details of carburetion."

Judith Evans watched her husband, hurting for him. The new engine had been his last hope of recouping his power. Now that this hope was gone, he still clung to the engine as some sort of symbol, as if seeing it make millions for the firm that had rejected him would somehow be an exoneration. Like posthumous medals, she thought.

He got up from the bed and walked to the window. The draperies were drawn against the light rain. He parted them and looked out, his dull eyes reflecting the shapes of the world that he and others like him had helped make. "They wouldn't vote the extra development funds," he said.

"They'll still go ahead, though," Judith told him. "It isn't as though the project were being shelved."

"No, they can't shelve it. Even Win Jenson can't turn his back on a project of this magnitude . . . with this much money in prospect."

"You've won, then. The engine will be introduced."

"Next year," he said bitterly. "Or the year after."

"But it *will* be produced."

"How do we know what other companies might be on the market by then with something similar? Given the basic research, anybody else with the tool-making capability could have a prototype inside six months. How can we sit back and take our good old time when time is so much of the essence in getting the jump on the market?"

"If they voted down the extra funds, Stan, it's out of your hands, isn't it?"

His shoulders slumped further. "I know. I'm through. As of tomorrow night, I'm out of it. I begin my illustrious retirement, complete with proxy voting of my stock, comprehensive medical care, generous monthly pension, and my picture in the 'emeritus' section of the annual report."

Hearing the scalding bitterness of his tired voice, she saw with renewed and painful clarity how much retirement was going to hurt him, and how savagely he had been beaten. Again she didn't say anything.

"I've put my life blood into that engine," he said, as if to no one. "I put my career on the line for it. It's going to change the face of American life, and Jenson could have been first with it, alone."

"They might still be first. They must think no one else is even close."

"That's what they think. The dumb bastards. The goddamned stupid bastards. They won't look ahead. They won't listen. They're going to be sorry."

Watching him, Judith felt a different kind of alarm. "Stan," she said wonderingly, "that sounds almost like a threat."

He turned to her. There was still fire underneath. Very deep, very much buried, very intense, smoldering. "Did it, Judith? How absurd."

"You look so tired, darling. Come over here." She moved to the bed. "Lie down with me a little while. Rest." She stretched out.

He came over slowly, removed his shoes, and extended his body on the bed beside her. His breathing had a bad rasp to it, and his breath was foul from countless cigarettes.

She wanted so much to help him.

"We'll have fun," she told him softly.

He said nothing.

"We can lie around and rest," she said. "And later, when we're both feeling better again, we can go to Mexico this winter."

"Yes."

"Remember when we went to Mexico before?"

"Yes, very well."

"The night on the balcony, after swimming?"

"Yes."

"We were silly and young then."

"I know."

"We can be silly again. We're not quite so young, but I think we're still just as silly, don't you?"

He took a deep breath. "I don't know."

"We'll have a wonderful time. You'll see."

"Good."

"You'll see us have a wonderful time and act as silly as we ever did."

"You know," he said slowly, "you can get tired in different ways. I guess I've been tired most of my life. I always told myself I could rest tomorrow, or the next day. Usually I did get some rest sooner or later, or some new project came along and I got charged up again and forgot about being tired."

"It will be that way again."

"I'm not so sure. It's different this time. There's a kind of tiredness that goes all the way through your bones and your being. You can't get rid of it by lying down for a while. It goes to your spirit. . . . I'm sorry if that sounds melodramatic."

"You'll be all right again," she said.

"Will I?"

"Yes."

"I hope so, Judith. But I don't think so."

She stared at the ceiling, trying to think of something to say. There wasn't anything. She was afraid. She kept her silence, stifling an impulse to cry. Good wives did not cry.

Using his pain-stiffened legs, Milo Rush managed to close the bathtub drain, and then tried awkwardly for over an hour to kick the cold water faucet on. Kenton's Run had good faucets. He couldn't even make this one drip.

He was still in darkness, his legs tied and his hands secured behind his back by the handcuffs. He had been so dazed at the time that he had not even realized it, but they had securely taped his mouth with wide adhesive. The best sound he could make was a groan. The bathroom walls were better than that.

The blow on the head, combined with the drug injection, had put him out for a long time. He knew this much. Judging by the dryness of his throat and the degree of pain in his body, it was now sometime in the evening. But after a period of numbness he was now fully aware of himself and the situation. He could remember some talk about how much of an injection to give him, and it appeared that he had been lucky. There was some fuzziness at the edges of his consciousness, and a lassitude now and then that could have been caused by either the blow or the injection. But he was far from unconscious.

For all the good it seemed to be doing him.

Lying cramped in the bathtub, he could see that he had been guilty of several serious miscalculations. He had misjudged the amount of help on the scene, their degree of desperation, and the timing of their plan. He had thought the act of sabotage or espionage would most likely come Friday night. This bad guess had made him less than fully prepared for their move to put him out of action tonight.

Assuming he stayed right where he was, the chances were excellent that he would be found tomorrow, late in the morning, when the maids came to make up the room. He could not assume that the men who had surprised him had any intention of coming back. Their masks and their use of a drug spoke too clearly of a single confrontation designed to keep him out of the way for a given brief time span, after which they would have vanished.

His job now was clear enough, but it looked impossible. They wanted him out of the way tonight. Therefore their job was planned for tonight. Therefore he had to get himself free if he was to have any chance of heading them off.

It was vital to head them off, because now he knew that Jane Clarken fitted directly into their scheme, and he thought he knew how. The only problem was the damned faucet that wouldn't budge. If he could get it going, he could keep his head above water while the tub overflowed. It might take an hour or two, but sooner or later the leakage into the room below would be reported.

Sweating heavily, he tried to kick the faucet some more. Nothing. Exhausted, he lay back against the cool porcelain and listened to his heart hammer.

There was a very slight chance that Les Montgomery might intercede, he thought. The telephone had rung for a long time, hours ago. Les might get concerned enough to come back on his own. As a matter of fact, the chances of this were very good. But even given perfect airline connections, it was three to four hours from the office in Washington to Kenton's Run. Usually airline connections were less than perfect. Assume Les kept trying on the telephone until, say, four o'clock. Assume he then went to the airport. Assume a plane out for Columbus between five and six—the best that could be hoped for. Add three and one-half hours, minimum. Nine. Possibly ten. More likely, eleven. Too late—and *that* was conjecture.

Rush sat up in the tub. He tried to heave himself against the side, to roll onto the floor. The tub was sunken and extra deep. He could not get himself turned around properly for the effort. A wave of nausea went through him, knocking him back to the bottom again.

For the first time he began seriously to consider the possibility that he was not going to get out of this in time, that he—and Jane Clarken—had had it.

The dining room orchestra began playing at 9:10, while Jane was still at the supper table with Jack Moradian and the Halsey couple. The Halseys were attending the sales-management sessions, Bud Halsey as a regional manager. He and his wife, Mary, were about the same age as Jane and Moradian, and the four of them had played one set of doubles on the tennis court a little earlier.

"The Stroganoff is good," Mary Halsey said. She was a small blonde with freckles and a constant smile. "How are the rest of you doing?"

"My steak—" Bud Halsey began.

"Pooh. I know how your and Jack's steaks are. Steaks are steaks. What I want to know about is Jane's lamb."

"It's excellent," Jane said. Which it was.

"We need another bottle of wine," Moradian observed, filling her glass.

"Where did *that* one go?" Mary asked.

"You drank it," Halsey said with a grin.

"Pooh!"

Moradian signaled to a waiter for another bottle of the mountain red, and Jane noticed the taut quality of his gesture. He was very busy trying to keep her glass filled, and she was not exactly protesting. She had a very slight buzz on. She needed it.

"More wine coming right up," Moradian told them.

"I'm glad we don't have an early start in the morning," Halsey said, "the way the wine has flowed so far."

"Just take it easy, sonny," Mary Halsey warned. "I feel like dancing."

Halsey ignored her and turned to Moradian. "So there won't be any announcements tomorrow, off-agenda?"

Moradian frowned for an instant. "No."

"I'm like everyone else, hearing these rumors about a big R and D program to be unveiled for us."

"It's been slowed down a little," Moradian said.

"How come?"

"Maybe we could talk about something more pleasant."

"Like that, huh? Listen—"

Mary Halsey leaned toward Jane. "If they're going to talk shop, I might as well take this chance to say I love your dress."

Jane glanced down at the new off-white dinner dress. It was cut low, revealing the tops of her golden breasts, and a slit skirt revealed leg when she walked. Yet its general cut was very plain, almost severe. She knew she looked good in it.

"Thank you," she said. "It's one my husband bought for me not long before the . . . accident."

Mary Halsey's eyes changed. "I was so sorry to hear about how you lost your husband. Such a tragedy!"

"Thank you," Jane said again, lowering her eyes.

Moradian and Halsey were still talking business.

"How long do you plan to stay here?" Mary asked.

"A few more days," Jane told her, lying again.

"We'll leave tomorrow afternoon, late."

"You won't attend the closing banquet?"

"Gee, we're not quite high up enough for that."

"Oh, I see."

"Yes, and we have to get back home to the kids. Gee, how I miss them!"

Jane smiled but didn't feel it. If she and Dave had had children by now, she thought, they might have provided a bulwark against people like Joe Graeber. But then she realized how bizarre this idea was—that children could protect parents.

Still, she had to find something . . . some basis for hope for the future. She had to arrange things, somehow, so Graeber could never again force her to do his bidding. She had to make sure no one else could appear in six months or a year—or ten years—and raise the specter of ruin for her marriage another time.

Sometimes she wondered if she could ever, even in decades, live it down. She would never forget. She had been an utter fool. But it had seemed so innocent at first, so easy. And she had felt so broke. At first it had been just fun, attending parties, acting partly as a social secretary, helping mix drinks, introducing people, being a kind of hostess. She had never known when it really first began to be more than that . . . when she first rode home with one of the men and liked him and was flattered, and finally let him stay the night . . . and then received the expensive watch in the mail at work.

Oh, at *some* point she had known. She had certainly known when Joe Graeber asked her to meet Boyce Oosterman, the computer company president, in Aspen at the lodge. Nothing specific had been said, but then nothing had been necessary. She had gone reluctantly, but she had gone. It had been very odd and very frightening, at first, meeting a man, and sleeping with him, when she had hardly known him before. But it was not so bad, really, because he had been reasonably attractive, very considerate, very generous. The payment at the home office had been in cash that time, as it would be in the future.

Still she might have turned back. Just because a brother died in Vietnam, girls all over the country didn't become part-time company call girls. But she had.

Not that she had thought of it that way until much later . . . until after the parties on the yacht, when only continual use of pot had helped to keep her going through with it . . . until after the investigation of the scandal, when she narrowly escaped with a resignation, and Joe Graeber's dismissal took him even nearer the federal courts.

That *had* frightened her, had made her see reason. She had gotten a more normal job, a straight one. Stopped drinking. Stopped pot. Became practically a hermit for a while. Began thinking it was all over, had a brief, unhappy affair, got through it, went on . . . finally met Dave.

Dave.

There was a chance, she knew, that he would see that something serious had taken place. He was a very intuitive man. She had her lies all ready, about the old girlfriend in deep trouble with drugs, about wanting to hide this from him if at all possible—a set of lies to "confess," after the first set of lies were proved transparent. Dave might be fooled . . . they might still have a chance. . . .

Which is more than they would have had if Joe Graeber had fulfilled his threat, proved with the pictures mailed to her, of telling Dave everything about her past, including names and positions and taped gasps, unless she agreed to go along on this one mission.

She had been so shocked by Graeber's blatant blackmail that she had left Washington in a daze. Now she found herself going through the motions with an automatic correctness, encouraging Jack Moradian while pretending sadness and aloofness. He wanted her now, obviously. The wine was part of his strategy for tonight. He was so transparent. It was clear to her that he was taking her seriously, and his intentions were not entirely male cynicism.

She wondered if any of it would have been easier if he had been a cynic.

Sitting at the table and conversing lightly with Mary Halsey, she continued to think beneath the surface of what was to happen later tonight, and then how she could get away tomorrow . . . face Dave . . . fight to save as much as she could . . . plan ways to protect herself from ever again being blackmailed. She was in agony. She told herself she had to take it a step at a time.

"Dessert, anyone?" Moradian asked after the meal was finished.

"I couldn't touch another bite!" Mary Halsey said, pressing a hand in on her dress under her pert breasts.

"Jane?"

She smiled, shook her head.

"After-dinner drinks, then."

They ordered. The orchestra came back from a break and began playing "Stardust."

"We have to dance to that," Moradian said.

Jane nodded assent and he led her onto the floor. Only a few other couples were dancing. She moved into his arms, acutely aware that it was the first time they had been quite this close, and found he was a good dancer.

"I don't want to go with them, do you?" Moradian said.

"Go? Where?"

"You heard Bud talking about taking a moonlight sailboat ride."

"I must not have been paying attention."

His hand on her back pressed lightly. "Preoccupied?"

"I guess so, Jack, yes."

"About me, I hope."

"About . . . a lot of things."

He turned her expertly through other couples, and they were free again. "We talked earlier about having some time to ourselves."

She said nothing. Her heart beat faster.

"Is that still all right?"

"Yes, Jack. Of course it is."

"I'll tell them we've decided to dance awhile longer, then. Encourage them to go on without us."

Again she said nothing.

"All right?"

"Yes."

"Then, after they've gone, we might run into somebody else right away. I mean, this place is crawling with Jenson types. And I do want to have you all to myself tonight."

She leaned back slightly to look at him. "But you just said you wanted to stay here, not go with them."

"I want to stay here long enough for them to leave. Then what would you say if I invited you up to my room?"

He asked hesitantly, uncertain of her. She was in tumult. But even as her mind raced over a dozen, a hundred, excuses and potentialities, she heard her voice replying very calmly.

"That would be nice," she said, "getting away from everyone."

He drew her slightly closer and she felt his masculine hardness against her. She thought of Joe Graeber and hated him. She also felt another gust of loathing, this one directed at herself. Against both she was helpless. *Just get through it,* she thought. *Just get through it. There's no other way.*

Eight

THE rain had passed through and the blacktop pavement was drying under pink-hued fluorescent lights a little after ten o'clock when a horse-drawn wagon pulled up in front of Kenton's Run. A small group of couples, perhaps a dozen, laughingly climbed aboard for the promised moonlight hayride. The wagon moved away lumberingly.

Other activities continued in a disorganized, desultory fashion. The lights beamed over the tennis courts, which were occupied. A handful of people splashed in the pool or sipped drinks on the patio. Someone had organized a night horseback ride around the lake, but the riders had split up on the way, regrouped more or less by accident, and now had a small fire burning on the far shore, the light yellow-red across the water. Tiny white lights showed two fishing boats were out. Inside the lodge, three men were playing snooker, a couple played Ping Pong, and half the tables remained occupied in the dining room, where the orchestra continued to play for dancing. In the TV lounge, a dozen persons sat in heavy chairs and watched the CBS "Thursday Night Movie." Steve McQueen was in it.

A station wagon pulled up at the far end of the parking lot and a bulky man got out, carefully locked the car, and walked to the cabana area, where he met another man in the shadows.

Judith Evans had managed to persuade her husband to go downstairs for supper after his nap, but they had arrived a trifle late and had to take a table alone. He was very quiet and withdrawn, and after a while she gave up trying to make conversation. He picked at his food. She watched some of the other couples dance and looked for a sight of Milo Rush. She did not see him. Again she wondered what had happened to him.

When they had finished eating, her husband reached for a cigarette and came up with an empty pack. He crumpled it wearily.

"The waiter can get some," Judith suggested.

"No," he said. "I have some more in the room."

"You want to go up now?" She was dismayed.

"Yes. I'm tired, Judith."

"We might have the waiter get you some. Then we could dance . . . just one."

He took a deep breath. "I suppose."

She saw how much it would cost him. "Never mind, dear. I'm tired too. Let's turn in."

Her new ivory dress moving stiffly against her skin, she walked with him through the lobby, to the elevators, upstairs to their room. The room smelled stale of cigarette smoke, to which her husband quickly added more. While he smoked, he silently undressed, went into the bathroom, brushed his teeth. Judith tried again to read a magazine. He came out of the bathroom, kissed her gently on the cheek, muttered a good night, and stretched across the bed.

For a little while he stared at the ceiling while she pretended to read. Then his breathing became more regular. He was asleep.

She put down the magazine and looked around the room. It was about 10:30. She felt edgy and upset. The prospect of staying in the room was unbearable. There would be others downstairs yet. She could find a group, possibly have just one drink, walk around.

Later she could bear the room, if she had the drink first and was more tired.

She went to the dresser and examined her reflection in the glass. The dress was perhaps cut a trifle young for her, but it nicely emphasized her mature breasts and swell of hips. Her eyes looked tired. But she was alive, she told herself. She was not old.

Letting herself out quietly, she went downstairs. To her dismay, the lobby was nearly deserted, and the few people around were not Jenson people. She took a few steps toward the sound of music in the dining room, then knew she could not go in alone and face the eyes she would meet. She veered off and stepped out onto the patio.

It was warmly humid and pleasant. The sound of splashing water in the pool echoed. The overhead lights were out, and the only illumination was from under the blue water itself.

She walked around the pool, touching her ivory shoes in the little black puddles in the pavement.

She stopped after making the circuit and told herself she might as well admit whom she was looking for.

It was not that she was adventuring, she told herself. She was not. She wanted only a friendly face, a nice voice, someone who seemed alive across the table for a drink. She wanted to stop thinking of how Stan's face looked, how his breathing sounded as he fitfully slept.

On impulse she turned back into the lobby and walked to the desk. The red-haired girl was on duty.

"Have you seen Mr. Rush this evening?"

"No, I sure haven't."

"Could you ring his room, please?"

"Yes, ma'am, if you'll just go to that house phone there."

Pulse murmuring, she listened to the telephone buzz. No need to tease or pretend, she thought. *I'll buy you a nightcap to prove the old lady isn't angry*, she would say.

"I'm sorry, Mrs. Evans. He doesn't seem to answer."

"All right. Thank you."

Feeling let down, she walked back outside again. She knew she was being very silly. The more she was alone, the more she *felt* alone.

Perhaps he was at the tennis courts.

She walked a little faster.

In Jack Moradian's room, Jane sat on the edge of the bed, legs crossed, and watched Moradian pour stiff drinks neat into water glasses. Despite the air conditioning, he was sweating. The silence between them had been getting heavier since their arrival moments earlier.

It would all unravel predictably, she thought. She had not

seen Milo Rush all afternoon, which meant he had either given up or was waiting to see what her game might be. It was too late for him to stop any of it now. She was no longer worried, only dully depressed, fighting to keep the self-hatred submerged.

Moradian brought her the drink and sat beside her. "There you are. Drink it all up like a good girl."

She looked over the glass at him. "It's a lot."

"It won't hurt you."

She sipped from the glass.

"There. You see?" His hand gently massaged her back.

She looked at him directly.

"And I won't hurt you either," he said.

"I know that, Jack."

"I like you very much. Do you know that, too?"

"Yes."

He took the glass from her hand, put it on the floor, and put his arms around her. She did not resist. He kissed her.

It was a very strange and almost frightening experience for her, being kissed by another man. It was not unpleasant, at least not yet. She had known it was coming and had prepared herself for it. When his tongue moved into her mouth, she parted her teeth and used her own tongue too, gently sucking. His arms tightened.

"See?" he whispered in her ear a moment later. "I haven't hurt you yet, have I?"

She clung to him, allowing his hand to slide under her arm. He found her breast and squeezed gently, then turned her head so he could kiss her again. He tried to bear her back across the bed with his weight.

"Jack," she gasped, "wait."

He stopped, watching her. His eyes betrayed a sudden fear that she was going to stop him.

"Could we please go to my little cabin? It just seems more private . . . and there's something there I need."

"Of course, darling. I understand. Shall we take our drinks along?"

She kissed his cheek. "I think I have quite enough stimulation already."

He stood. "I'll just bring mine along."

She walked to the draperies of the windows that looked out across the deck and down toward the pool area. She grasped the pull cords and opened the curtains. "I just want to make sure we won't be seen—will you turn off the light, so I can step out and make sure?"

He grinned. "Afraid of what people will say?" But he complied, cutting the switch at the wall and plunging the apartment into darkness.

"Of course I am," she said, pretending to look over the patio area from the balcony.

"Satisfied?" he said when she went back inside.

"Yes," she replied, startled as he almost roughly took her in his arms again.

"Let's go to your house," he said after a minute. His voice was husky.

"All right."

"Did you lock that balcony window again?"

"Yes, of course."

He left her for a moment, and she heard the closet door open and close as he evidently put the portfolio case out of sight. She moved to the front door, waiting. His hands found her. He held her against the door. She let his hands move. *I just can't stand it. . . .*

"Ready?" he said.

"Yes."

He opened the door onto the lighted hallway, which was deserted. With a conspiratorial wink he took her hand and led her down the back stairway. It was 10:45.

Finishing her drink on the patio, Judith Evans watched the last two swimmers climb out of the pool, faintly gleaming, and walk toward the cabana. She was entirely alone at her end of the patio, one of only four or five people remaining to press the boundary of the sign that said the pool area was closed at 11 P.M. By her watch she saw that she had only eight or nine minutes remaining.

The eleven o'clock deadline would be a stimulus, she thought. Nowhere else to go, little old lady. Toddle off.

Breathing deeply, she looked around the area, up at the dim

walls of the hotel, across the pool and golf course and lake to the distant lumpy shapes of the Ohio hills. There had been a time when the word "retirement" connoted rural scenes to her—a country home, ease and grace, time for a garden and evenings on a lawn, and love. The actual prospect now was desolate.

She wondered again about Milo Rush. He had not been seen since morning. It did not seem normal for him to be completely out of sight over this period. Of course, she thought, he might have business here that she knew nothing about . . . might have gone off to some other lodge or town.

He might also, she thought suddenly, be sick.

It was a stupid idea, but the moment it came to her, it seemed to make terrifyingly good sense.

He hadn't mentioned going anywhere today. She thought she could recall their discussing the possibility of tennis in the afternoon. He had intended to be here. But he wasn't.

. . . Unless, she thought, again suddenly, he was in his room . . . had been in his room all day.

Men had sudden illnesses. Hearts failed. He *could* have had such a thing happen to him.

She knew the notion was absurd and hysterical. But as she sat there imagining it—he on the floor of his room, unconscious, possibly dying, the telephone ringing, no one to come see where he was—the fear bit deeper into her bloodstream. He probably was just fine. The chances were a million to one against a bad accident. But it *was* possible . . . it could have happened. . . .

Her nerves, already frayed, strung tighter as she sat very still and thought about it. Absurd! she decided.

She got up and went back into the lobby. "Will you try Mr. Rush's room again for me, please?"

Again there was no response.

She sighed, decided she was a fool, and got into the elevator. But as she reached for the button, on impulse again, she punched 3.

She knew his room number. She walked to the door, which of course was closed. She looked around, saw no one, and, feeling an utter fool, knocked.

There was no response, only a distant sound like someone tapping on a wall. She wondered where the workmen were busy at this hour. It sounded as if it might be a floor away, someone rapping with a hammer or tool made of hard rubber, perhaps to loosen some recalcitrant appliance.

Which was when she got a chill.

Workmen didn't tap appliances in a hotel, and the sound, now that she listened hard for it, was not that far away.

She bent to the door and knocked again, harder, and listened. The clapping sound came from inside.

"Milo?" she called.

The sound perhaps intensified, something dense being hit with a curiously sluggish rhythm against a hard surface, possibly a wall.

And it was inside.

She was sure of that.

She ran for the elevator.

Daugherty had been waiting on the fourth-floor landing, and when his tiny walkie-talkie beeped at him, he quickly removed the instrument from his belt and dropped it behind the heating-cooling unit protruding from the buff-colored wall. The camera and flashgun in his coat pocket bumped softly against his hip as he moved through the door to the next flight of stairs and took them two at a time, his heavy thigh muscles straining with haste.

At the fifth floor he shot an exploratory glance through the wire-woven glass in the fire door and went swiftly into the corridor. It was quiet and a little musty. Taking the stolen key from his pocket, he walked directly to the room he wanted, unlocked the door, and stepped confidently inside. He pocketed the key again and sprayed the penlight into the darkness.

Barring something wholly unforeseen, it was going to be a very quick and easy piece of work. He thought fleetingly of the girl snoozing in a room below. He would be back beside her before she roused to know he had ever been gone, he thought. Then they would celebrate, although she would not realize it was a celebration.

The penlight's narrow cone of illumination rested on the portfolio case. Daugherty knelt beside it, opening the soft leather folder of lock-picking tools on the floor.

"My *God!*"

The bathroom light, suddenly flicked on, partially blinded Milo Rush after the many hours of pitch blackness. It was Jenny, the girl who worked behind the desk, in the doorway. But the exclamation had come from Judith Evans, who had gotten the first glimpse of him as she walked into the cubicle and pushed back the shower curtain.

"You were right," Jenny said grimly, kneeling beside the tub to start picking at the edge of the tape across Rush's mouth.

"He's been hurt!" Judith groaned.

"It's no heart attack, anyway. And I thought you were hysterical when you insisted—"

"You can't get the tape off that way. Here." Judith leaned across, grabbed an edge, and ripped it back.

Rush gasped at the hot pain. "Have you got a knife or something? Can you free my legs?"

"He's handcuffed behind his back!"

Jenny nodded. "Do you have anything in your purse we could use on these ropes?"

"I've got a nail file—"

"Try that." Jenny scrambled to her feet. "I'm going to have to call downstairs."

"Find Barry Timmerman," Rush said hoarsely. "Get him up here fast."

"We have a security man of our own. I'm going to call him, too."

"All right. If you have anybody on maintenance duty, they might have a hacksaw. Hurry!"

Jenny went into the bedroom, and a light flicked on. Judith bent over Rush's legs, struggling to get the point of the flimsy file into one of the knots. "Who did it, Milo? When? Why?"

"Long story," Rush told her. "I'm glad you decided to come looking for me."

"I tried to call earlier."

"I know. I heard it."

"If I had just thought—!"

"How could you guess? I'm lucky you came when you did. We might all still be lucky. What time is it?"

"I don't know—almost eleven—"

"Are you doing any good there?" He leaned forward awkwardly, trying to see.

"I've got one knot almost out."

Jenny could be heard talking on the telephone in the bedroom. Then she came back. "I don't know what's going on. I can't raise Timmerman, and our man doesn't answer his page device. But I've got the maintenance man on the way. I explained. He said he has some big bolt cutters."

"We'll just see how big they are," Rush grunted. "Most cuffs are tougher than any cutters, but maybe we'll be lucky."

"What happened?" Jenny was pale, but getting control.

"Call the police or the sheriff or whoever you've got around here. If you can't find Timmerman or your man, find the manager or anybody available. Get Jenson if you have to. Get some people up to Jack Moradian's room. Do you know the number, Judith?"

"No," she said, unraveling the heavy cords. "I—"

"I'll get it," Jenny said.

"If he's there, check the portfolio case," Rush ordered. "If he isn't, see if the case is gone too. Hunt for him."

Judith looked up. "They're after the—?"

"The ropes. Get my legs free, will you?"

Jenny said, "I don't know what's going on, but—"

"Do what I said!" Rush snapped. "And look for Mrs.—Hendrix, too. Moradian might be with her. Check her cabin."

Jenny stared at him a moment, uncomprehending, but then turned and fled from the room.

Judith pulled the cords free from his ankles. "There."

With the rush of stronger circulation, Rush's legs felt as if they had caught fire. He struggled to get up, the handcuffs still rendering his arms helpless behind him. Seeing his effort, Judith tried to help. He got his legs under his body and pushed up. He got to his feet and started to step up onto the floor. The sudden change of position sent a wave of dizziness through him. He crashed heavily to the floor, knocking over a metal wastebasket.

"Milo—!"

Tasting blood, he managed to heave himself up to a sitting position. He asked her for water. With trembling hands she fed him. He realized that he might still be feeling the aftereffects of the drug as well as the confinement. His near vision was fuzzy and he could not get all his thoughts organized perfectly.

"Milo, what happened? Why did they do this to you? They're after the engine plans, is that it?"

"That's it, babe," Rush muttered.

"And you knew—?"

"I wandered around this place like a jackass, only half-tumbling to what was going on. Then I guessed wrong on their timing."

"They could have killed you."

It was the kind of comment that required no reply. "Where's your husband?"

"Up in the room, asleep—"

"Go wake him. Tell him what's happened. He'll know what to do."

The maintenance man walked into the bedroom and looked in at them. He was an old man with a toolbox in one hand and an enormous set of bolt cutters in the other.

Rush looked at the five-foot handles. "Maybe," he said with satisfaction.

"Looks like you're in a fix," the old man said, putting down the toolbox.

"Milo," Judith said, "do you want me to leave you and go tell—"

"Yes. Hurry!"

She limped out of the room. The heel on one of her shoes had broken off.

"If you want to shinny around a mite," the maintenance man said, "I figger I can get some leverage in this direction."

Rush complied. The old man fixed the cutting jaws to the chain of the cuffs, resting the bit on the tile floor. He pressed back on the end of the raised handles and tried to squeeze them. "Uuunh!"

"That won't work. You'll have to get one handle on the floor and use your weight."

"Man, I got these to cut an old dumbwaiter chain. Them handcuffs is tough."

"They're supposed to be."

The man rearranged the cutters, their cold jaws touching

Rush's wrists. He threw his weight on the upright handle, and the jaws bit into the hard steel. A link snapped loudly. "There's one of 'em!"

Rush waited impatiently while the jaws were readjusted. He had no idea whether he was in time. The fact that Jenny had been unable to raise either Timmerman or the lodge's own security man sounded bad. Except for the maintenance man's asthmatic breathing, there was no sound, but that meant nothing: a building of this size could absorb a great deal of noise even if there was some on another level. And Rush had been very near the site of a major jewel theft once. The entire operation had taken place in the quiet of a tomb.

He had plenty of time to think about it, and of course now it all seemed perfectly clear. Jane Clarken was to get Moradian out of the way, and the others were to steal or photograph the engine plans and specifications. Development projects were not protected by patent, because, more often than not, they used existing patents in original configurations. Rush knew that Jenson was not anywhere near production of whatever its engine design might be. Another company might make a quantum jump entirely ahead of Jenson, given the present planning and a greater production capacity. Things like that had happened before. The claim always was that the other firm had developed its program independently. Different engineers had come up with simultaneous, separate developments before, hadn't they? The problem of pollution was no secret. What was more normal than two or even three firms' coming up with similar solutions at almost the identical time? What could anyone ever prove? Even records of past studies, to be shown the curious as proof of long-term development, could be faked. That had been done before, too.

The bolt cutters snapped the remaining link of the handcuffs. Pain stabbed Rush's back muscles as he moved his freed arms.

"Looks like that ought to do it until we can use the hacksaw on the bracelets," the old man said, grinning.

Moving sore arms, Rush got unsteadily to his feet. "Thanks."

"You want to come in here and we'll saw on them bracelets now?"

"Later." Rush went into the bedroom and pulled his suitcase

down. He got out the revolver and shoved it into his pants pocket. He was still dizzy and slightly nauseated, but he left the room and went into the hallway, which was quiet and deserted.

His footsteps sounded soft as he hurried down toward the elevator. "Mr. Rush?"

He turned to see a tall, lanky man in a dark summer suit coming out of the stairwell. He had seen him downstairs in the lobby.

"I'm Jones," the man said excitedly. "The manager. Jenny said—"

"We need your security man up on five, and we need him fast," Rush told him. "Have you found Timmerman?"

"It's all right, Mr. Rush. Everything is all right. Say, you've had a nasty bump on the head, too. We'll go down to the first-aid station—"

"What do you mean, it's all right?" Rush demanded.

Jones looked excited, but his smile was self-satisfied. "We've headed it off, sir. Mr. Timmerman and our Mr. Shea have everything well in hand. If you want to come down to the office, I expect the sheriff will be arriving directly."

"You got there in time, then?"

Jones beamed. "The culprit is in custody, sir. Come with me and see for yourself. Under the circumstances, I'm sure you want to do just that."

There was a small commotion in the lobby near the registration desk. Judith was there, with her husband, who was wearing a bathrobe, and a couple of people Rush did not know. Jenny stood nearby, very pale. The door to the manager's office was closed, and Win Jenson stood beside it, hands in the pockets of his rumpled slacks. He looked as if he had just been awakened, or had been drinking heavily.

As Jones walked up with Milo Rush, Jenson turned angrily to meet them. "Jones? See here! I demand a full explanation! I demand the right to interrogate—"

"In good time, sir," Jones said smoothly. "Excuse me?" With surprising ease he maneuvered Rush past the startled Jenson and into the office, closing the door behind them.

There were three others in the small, utilitarian office. Sitting in a straight chair against the wall, glum and sullen, was the beefy man Rush had seen trying to bully the girls at the desk the first day. Barry Timmerman stood beside the small metal desk. Behind the desk stood a somewhat older Timmerman copy, red-haired, freckled, wearing a loud sports shirt with a shoulder holster incongruously strapped across it.

"Hello, Mr. Rush," Timmerman said, his forehead wrinkling heavily. "We got him."

"I'm Shea," the other one behind the desk said. "I guess he didn't want you around, from what Jenny said. Right?"

"Who is he?" Rush snapped.

"Well, there are two schools of thought on that," Timmerman replied quietly. "He's registered as Henry Walters. His billfold says his name is Daugherty. I guess you can believe what you want."

Beyond the venetian blinds at the window there was a fluttering of red and white lights. Tires squealed on pavement.

"Sheriff's here," Shea said.

Timmerman told Rush, "We've got somebody on the door of Moradian's room, and I've sent a man down to that tree house to see if he's with Mrs. Hendrix. Or whatever *her* real name is. Is she in this deal with this guy?"

"I don't know," Rush lied. "Maybe not—"

"He stole a room key from behind the desk," Timmerman said calmly. "That is, the extra key disappeared, so the girls told the manager, who routinely notified Shea, here. When he passed it on to me, I began to put two and two together. Mrs. Hendrix was up in Moradian's room as recently as forty-five minutes ago. I was watching the corridor. They left and went outside, I figure to her place. Then our friend here came up the back stairwell and used his stolen key to get right in." Timmerman nodded toward the desk, on the top of which were strewn a camera, flashgun, key, extra film package, folded leather case of lock-pick tools and small flashlight. "He was getting right with it when we went in on him."

"What's his story?"

"No story. He—"

The office door opened and a short, rotund man in Levis, a faded blue shirt and a straw hat came in, followed by a strapping boy with a badly sunburned face. The older man had a police special belted high on the right side.

"What's all this about, now?" he asked.

Rush took the opportunity to step back outside, into the area behind the desk. Everyone was still there, and coming across the lobby from the pool doors, with a youth Rush did not know, were Moradian and Jane. They were pale, their eyes at pinpoints from the sudden glare. Moradian's shirttail was not all the way in, and bare ankles flashed under his trousers as he walked. Jane's hair was down, flowing, her makeup smudged. Her dress was shapeless and rumpled in a way that said it had been thrown on quickly, with nothing underneath. She was barelegged, her feet in sandals.

As they came to the desk, she saw Rush. For a second their eyes met. The look was a physical blow for him, because he needed no more. He had thought it might not be too late, at least not too late to prevent that. Now he knew otherwise.

"Milo—?" she said. But he brushed past her and the dazed Moradian and headed for the pool doors.

Outside in the humid darkness he leaned his head against the glass and tried to get himself back together. Everything was flowing too swiftly, and he was still dazed, probably from the drug. Daugherty, or whatever his name was, had not been one of the men who had been waiting in his room. But Timmerman and Shea had not found them with Daugherty when they made the arrest. Those two, then, were still loose. By now they could be in the next county.

Daugherty would take the rap, then. And possibly Jane. But they really couldn't pin anything on Jane. They did not put people in jail much for adultery anymore. Unless Daugherty talked—which seemed unlikely, because he looked like an old pro and a hard case—Jane was perfectly in the clear as far as charges were concerned.

Maybe Daugherty simply hadn't checked things clearly enough, Rush thought. Overlooking a follow-up on the stolen key had been extremely stupid, unlike a man who went to great lengths to find and blackmail a woman, bring her here, set her up at great cost to lure Moradian away at precisely the right time. It was almost as if Daugherty himself had been set up.

With that thought, Rush's head snapped up and suddenly felt very clear.

"Jesus Christ," he whispered.

Everything looked the same in the lobby. People looked startled as he pushed past them to get to the closed office door. Evans tried to say something to him. Rush ignored him and bolted inside.

Everyone in the small office turned.

"Barry," he said, "you've got a man outside Moradian's room?"

"Right," Timmerman said slowly. "It's locked securely, and—"

"Get his ass *inside* the room," Rush ordered. *"Right now."*

Without waiting for a response, he turned and ran for the stairwell.

Nine

THE moon, orange through patchy clouds, faintly illuminated the geometric clutter of the roof as Milo Rush opened the steel security door and stepped out onto the graveled surface. He was badly out of breath. Air-conditioning units, like stacks of rough lumber, stood taller than his head, along with cylindrical vents, boxy wiring areas and an irregular line of exhaust pipes. They blocked his view toward the near edge of the flat roof.

He moved along the side of the roaring air-conditioning tower, came to its corner, and looked around it. Just as he did so, distantly, he heard what sounded like a gunshot. From far below somewhere there were men's shouts. The chance for a cautious approach was lost.

Moving into full view, he looked across a thirty-foot expanse of white gravel roof studded here and there by small protruding pipes. The edge of the roof was built up about a foot, making a pale wall against the drop-off beyond. The first thing he saw was a coil of rope near the wall. Then, following the wall with his eyes, he saw the glint of metal on the edge—a lightweight grappling hook firmly attached, with a line extending over the top and evidently down the side of the building on its west side.

Rush reached for his gun and started forward.

A bulky figure appeared from behind one of the fat vent pipes nearby. Rush had time to get general impressions—a white shirt open at the collar, pumping legs in dark trousers, a thick pale face and an arm raised. The man had been close to start with, and now was charging him. The revolver hung up in his pants pocket. He saw some sort of club in the man's hand. He ducked to the right, toward the edge of the roof. The man veered with him, hitting him in the midsection with a football shoulder block.

Rush's wind was driven from him and he staggered backward. The parapet caught his legs near the knees. He was going over backward. The man who had hit him was now sprawled fully forward on the gravel roof at his feet, but this was no advantage, because his own balance was gone. Panic gusting through him, he clawed at the air, fighting to regain his balance. He managed to turn his body in the air so that his hip smashed the little wall as he went over.

His left hand smacked the retaining edge momentarily, losing flesh, but he could not maintain any sort of grip. He was over the edge and done for. His breath went out of him and he fell.

For just an instant there was a rush of wind and total disorientation. Then he hit something with a stunning impact and a tremendous crashing sound. He felt wood or plastic explode all around him before he bounced and came to rest and rolled over, groggy.

Miraculously, he had fallen a dozen feet onto the sixth-floor balcony of one of the rooms. The wreckage of a table was strewn all around him. He had hit it and demolished it. His head clearing, he managed to sit up and ascertain that nothing major was broken.

The wall—sliding glass doors—lighted up brightly beside him. He heard a man's voice demanding to know what had happened. The draperies shot open to reveal a bedroom, rumpled bed, gray carpet, dresser, mirror, clothes tossed around, a woman sitting up with a sheet clutched to her throat, a man in garish pajamas fumbling with the catch of the sliding door.

Below somewhere on the ground there was more shouting.

Rush scrambled to his feet as the big, bald-headed man slid the door back. "What the hell is going *on* out—?"

"Sorry," Rush muttered, and bolted past him into the room. The woman screamed, right out of the Keystone Kops. Rush ignored her and headed for the far door. The man yelled hoarsely, but Rush was already through the door and into the hall.

The stairwell entry at the far end of the corridor was empty. He paused but couldn't hear anything over his own tattered breath. Finally getting his revolver clear, he started down as fast as he could go. The stairs were well insulated, and the only sound was his own, which was considerable.

There was no time to put any of it in order, but he now understood what had happened. Daugherty, whether he had known it or not, had been a decoy. His arrest had only served to provide the commotion necessary for the real burglary. Judging by the sounds at ground level, the man on the roof had been only one of a team entering Moradian's guarded apartment with a rope from above. Maybe Timmerman or someone else had caught the other man or men. Problematical. All Rush knew was that his own quarry was probably ahead of him somewhere, getting the hell out as fast as possible.

Reaching the first-floor landing, he tried the basement door and found it locked. There were two other doors, one leading into a darkened kitchen area, and also locked, and the other going outside. Rush went outside.

He found himself on a small concrete porch with three steps leading down to a sidewalk that led through some tall evergreens. Beyond the trees was a wider sidewalk going along the side of the building. To the left was a steep embankment, rocks, and thick vegetation. He went right. The sidewalk took him out to the northwest corner of the lodge. The parking lot was still under softly glowing pole lamps. He could look along the east, toward the front entrance where the sheriff's car still sat with its roof lights rotating red and white. He couldn't see anyone.

Running footsteps sounded behind him. He whirled. A figure appeared out of the darkness, gun in hand. "Hold it right there!" the voice called.

Rush didn't move as Barry Timmerman, also out of breath, ran up beside him.

"You, Mr. Rush? Did you find somebody?"

"There was one on the roof. He got away."

"The one in Moradian's room didn't. I heard some yelling and maybe shots out back, too. I don't know what's going on, but we've got the one, anyway."

"I thought my man would break for the outside. I don't see him."

Timmerman pointed. "He could have gone down into that brush."

"He might have gone into the hotel, too. He might be a registered guest."

"Shit. Right. He could be back in a room by now." Timmerman brushed the back of his hand across his sweat-soaked forehead. "I'm going to get out back and see what's going on out there." He turned and ran back the way he had come, his heavy footsteps fading into silence.

Rush remained in the shadows of the big evergreens. If his man from the roof was a registered guest, he thought, there was no chance to catch him through pursuit. But it was also possible that an intruder might coolly cut back through the hotel, catch his breath, and walk out the front door just as if nothing had happened.

Waiting for this possibility, Rush felt reaction to his fall from the roof begin to set in. His body had been so battered in the past dozen hours that his reaction time was abnormally slow. His legs began to go a little weak and he felt nauseated again. He knew he could just as easily have fallen *between* balconies the entire six floors to the ground. Thinking about that, he forced himself to breathe slowly and deeply and let the weakness spread.

He felt a gnawing desire to confront the man from the roof. It was possible that the planner of the operation was nowhere nearby at all. But if the ringleader had been in the operation itself, the chances were excellent that the roof man had been that ringleader. A man on ground level, if there had been one, was a lookout, probably with a radio. The man who went down the rope to the fifth floor balcony was a specialist. The roof man was the one in position to see everything and call for changes. He was also the one with the most difficult potential escape route, assuming the man in the room could exit into the hall. The bulky man who had been on the roof, then, was a crucial factor in getting the answers that Rush badly wanted.

He decided to give it another five minutes in his present

position, then walk to the front entry, where he could watch both the lobby and the parking lot awhile longer. The roof man had no way of knowing whether he had been recognized clearly enough for identification; he was not likely to remain on the scene any longer than necessary. There was also the panic factor. Rush knew how strong that could be in any man.

Several minutes ticked away.

When Rush first saw him, he was already well away from the building and in the parking lot. He was walking fast between rows of cars, carrying a small suitcase of some kind. The white shirt was the same, the size of his shoulders was the same, and the hairline was the same.

Rush stepped out of hiding and started across the pavement toward him.

The man turned, his face flashing. Rush broke into a run. The man jerked open the door of a dark-colored Ford station wagon and threw the suitcase inside, then jumped behind the wheel. The door slammed and the engine fired simultaneously. Rubber shrilled as the wagon backed out, then smoked again as the driver cranked the wheel hard, rocketing the car toward the far end of the lot and the road beyond.

Up on the road beyond were faint yellow lights, bobbing along. The hayride wagon coming back.

Rush veered direction and headed for his own rental car. The slot in front of it was empty, so he could drive straight out. He got in and turned the ignition key. The starter whined but did not catch. Cursing all pollution controls, Rush tried again, pumping the accelerator.

Up at the curving intersection of parking lot driveway and narrow country road, the brake lights on the Ford suddenly flared red. There was a puff of dust and some sort of gravel spray. The Ford skewered around in the roadway beside the hay wagon, then straightened out and pulled onto the road, heading uphill around the corner.

Rush got the engine started and floorboarded it unmercifully. It missed, backfired, and then took hold. The back end slewed around as he swung past the other parked cars and pounded down the incline to the road exit, getting headlights on.

The hay wagon was pulled well to the side of the road, and

the driver was down in the roadway looking at the left rear wheel of the wagon. It did not appear damaged, but there were gravel and dirt on the pavement, and a retaining post had been sheared off at the edge of the ditch. Faces flashed white as Rush's headlights caught them. He did not slow down any more than necessary, and, once past the wagon, jammed the accelerator to the floor. The Chevrolet began to get the message. It backfired once through the carburetor, ritualistically, and then seemed to flatten out on the smooth blacktop, screaming as speed built up.

Topping the rise where the road turned back upon itself to climb a hill, Rush had a brief moment to look ahead. The road was snakelike through the hills, ravines and rock formations, and up ahead perhaps a half-mile he could see the spray of headlight glow against trees. He knew his own headlights would tip off his pursuit. There was no help for that; no one could drive this crazy road by the pale moonlight.

Sawing the wheel sharply, he negotiated a hundred-degree turn and then plunged down a steep little hill and over a bridge. On the far side, the road twisted up to the left, rising sharply, with rocks bright yellow in the headlights. He used the gear selector to get more torque, not worrying about what he might do to engine or tires in the process.

He realized that his seat-belt buzzer was yammering, and the bright red light flashed on the instrument panel. With his free hand, he jerked the belt out of the floor receptacle and twisted it back to silence the warnings. It might have been nice to use the belt, he thought, but in the process of buckling it he would have gone off the twisting road.

A glance in the rear-view mirror told him no one else was in pursuit. They would come. The people from the hay wagon would report what they had seen, and someone would add it up. But that would take a minute or two. Too long, Rush thought. If the man in the Ford was going to be caught, it was up to him alone.

The road momentarily straightened, sliding down the side of a black hill, and he saw the speedometer bounce over 70. Then the sharp curve sign flashed by, and he had to lock all four wheels to slide through the hairpin, almost losing it. The engine screamed complaint going up the other side in intermediate range, and at the top there was a hump that put all four wheels airborne for a sickening instant before the galumphing crash of hitting down again.

The other car was on the next hill, clearly visible, closer, not more than a quarter-mile now. Hitting the post might have done something to the Ford's suspension, because the driver had to know he was being chased by now, yet he was losing ground fast.

Everything else was pitch black. The road had been cut out of the hills for use by sightseers and tourists and was just wide enough for two vehicles. Sliding wide on a tight curve, Rush tried not to imagine what it would be like if someone met him from the other direction. That uncertainty was worse for the other man, he thought with satisfaction.

Nobody could be allowed to get away. It might not matter, now, ultimately. The expression in Jane Clarken's eyes still seared him. It might be fashionable to have a more liberated view of things—he could remember the woman in his office calmly telling him that she didn't know why her husband was so concerned, "It was just a casual fuck"—but Jane had never been that liberated; Dave Clarken had never been that liberated either. She had left him and come here and gone to bed with Jack Moradian, and that was *not* casual, not for her, not for Dave, not ever. There was no way this could be truly hidden from Dave; he would know. Nothing was ever going to be quite the same again. They might never make it up. Something might have died.

Rush knew with a part of himself that this was illogical. But he knew his people. That was why he was driving with a kind of fury. He wanted all of them. He wanted to know *why*. It might not help. He wanted it anyway, even if the hope was slim.

The Chevrolet shuddered from end to end as he drifted through another sharp turn. He was beginning to get the feel of the big car, making it obey the way small cars did in road racing. It was badly sprung, much too soft, and the steering very imprecise, like all big Detroit cars. But he was beginning to learn how it shuddered when it was really going to break loose, and was making use of the knowledge. He could feel the car at all levels now, was one with it. Rock embankments and brushy overhangs flashed by the headlights. Sweat stung his eyes despite the cool night wind gushing through the opened side window. He saw taillights ahead and knew he had gained again.

They were not far now from the edge of the forestry area. Beyond, the scenic route intersected a better, straighter state road. He saw that he was not going to catch the Ford prior to that. Without thinking about it, he pressed the accelerator, increasing his chances of losing all traction on the pavement. The tires howled, but he held the pressure, teasing the steering wheel back and forth for maximum control. Once the Ford reached the state road, it could be a new ballgame. There was no way to know which car might be faster on a surface with fewer curves and hills.

Through the curved windshield, Rush could see that the clouds overhead seemed thinner. The moon presently beamed full out of a long rift between cigar-shaped dark masses. He could see down a long valley to his left, off the side of the hill, and the moonlight shone on dark trees unbroken by any sign of habitation.

The red heat indicator on the instrument panel began to flicker.

Topping the hill, Rush had to saw the wheel hard left as the road turned back upon itself, and then, just as he began to regain full control, the road dropped off sharply and twisted again, first to the right and then back to the left. He remembered the section; it was less than a mile to the state road intersection. He looked ahead but could not see any other lights.

He was soaked in sweat now. His arms had begun to ache sharply from the constant struggle with the wheel. The Chevrolet had power steering, but continual changes of direction threw him around on the seat, and he was using considerable strength to hang on and exert leverage. He had given up even the slimmest pretext of anything but pursuit: he was driving on high beams only, trying to get every foot of road illumination possible. The pitching of the softly sprung sedan sent the lights high against trees and rock walls, then hard down against the black pavement, in a crazy seasick pattern.

He tunneled down a slanting curve, bottomed out, his head crashing against the inside roof, and spun the wheel sharply to stop an incipient skid. Then, magically, a stone gate formation —entry to the wilderness area—flashed past on the right, and the road swept down again, the curve becoming gentle. The speedometer swept up past 60 and the tires squealed against the wooded curve, and he saw, a quarter-mile ahead, the bright lights of the Ford's back end, braking. It was the state road intersection. The Ford turned right and gunned out hard. It either fishtailed or shimmied, going away under the moonlight.

Rush rode the brakes hard as he approached the stop sign and, seeing no other cars, drifted into the turn at high speed. The front end bottomed out with a jarring crash as the wheels hit the slightly higher pavement ridge, but then he caught the back end coming around and straightened out with power, shifting the selector into the top range. The Chevvie responded nicely.

Up ahead the Ford was in trouble. It swerved to the far side of the two-lane road, swept back erratically and hit the shoulder. It started to go all the way around. Rush got off the accelerator and onto the brake because he saw that this was a slide the Ford would not recover from.

For an instant he saw the Ford go on around, skidding sideways, something flying off—a hubcap—in a spray of gravel and dirt. Then the Ford was going backward, smoke erupting from under the hood as the engine blew, and then it was down in the ditch beside the low, flat cornfield, with a hill vaulting up blackly a hundred yards away. Then Rush was too busy fighting his own car to see what the other one was doing.

He skidded with all four wheels locked, the noise earsplitting, the car trying to turn on him as he spun the wheel first left, then right. The front tire hit gravel and dug in, and he let up a little, but by then he was enveloped by the smoke and sifting dirt from the Ford's wreck into the ditch, and he couldn't see what was going on. The Chevvie slowed and then lurched to a stop, its engine dying.

For a split second Rush sat behind the wheel, staring into the whirling maelstrom of dust and smoke illuminated by the headlights. It was quiet.

Then he punched out the lights, got his door open, and rolled out onto the hot pavement. He crawled to the front of his car, getting his gun out and ready, and peered around through the smoke.

The Ford was nose-down in the ditch fifty paces away. Fire licked at the shattered hood. The driver's side door was open. Rush couldn't see anyone. He hesitated.

Something cracked softly—wood breaking. He turned his head slightly and saw his man going over the rickety barbed-wire fence near a post which his weight had evidently shattered. The man had something in his hand. A gun.

"Hold it!" Rush called.

The man pitched over the fence and rolled in the soft earth. But he got his legs under him swiftly and churned into the shoulder-high corn.

Rush thought he could catch him by moving swiftly. Leaving the safety of his car's shadow, he ran low and zigzagged for the ditch. From the corn something spanged loudly, hollow, and a bullet buzzed wickedly over his head. He hit the ditch in a face-first dive and came up spitting mud and weeds. The mud was shockingly cold.

Climbing through the ditch, he crawled under the fence, snagging his arm painfully in the process. He lay still for a moment, feeling the cool earth soak into his clothes and body. His eyes were beginning to adjust, but he could see only the pale cornstalks, in close rows, and the dark sky with the moon well overhead. A wispy fog over the field made horizontal vision more difficult.

It was a very bad situation now. He thought briefly about turning back. It might be his last chance to make absolutely certain of finding out everything about Jane Clarken's involvement. That was the one thing he could not afford to miss.

The corn was drying. About thirty or forty feet directly ahead of him, it rustled. Making his decision, he started crawling down the row, trying to keep his movements as quiet as possible. Creepers tugged wetly at him, and he smelled rotten vegetation, mud and manure.

There were times when Milo Rush was reminded vividly how isolated from physical reality his life rendered him. He was more active than most. But walking down a golf course fairway was totally unlike this experience. This took him back to Germany, during one of the many exercises, when the assignment was abstract but the bullets were real. The body quickly forgot the shock of cold mud against the pores, the smells of the earth, the sound of breath rasping in the lungs, the coppery taste of fear. But it was all back with him now as he slogged cautiously, on elbows and hips.

A field mouse scuttered in fright from his path.

Pausing to keep his breathing as controlled as possible, Rush listened intently. There was no sound except the distant hum of night insects. Mud itched between his fingers. He wanted very badly to get back out of this damned field now. The revolver in his hand was scant consolation. He had no way of knowing how expert his man might be, but he suspected the worst. Crawling around in a muddy southern Ohio cornfield was just about as stupid as anything he had ever done.

A slight sound off to the right made his hair prickle on the back of his neck. He strained his eyes but couldn't see anything except the cornstalks and black sky with wispy fog just over his head. He began to shake. This was not fear but the body reacting in its own way to the entire series of shocks. His cells were talking to him now. He had plunged himself backward in time to an elemental level, and his senses were becoming more acute in primordial ways. He could hear his own heartbeat and the slight rasp of his breathing.

He edged forward again, going against the things his cells were trying to tell him.

It was normal for fright to tug strongly, telling him to panic and run. He knew this. But as he stopped and lay still again, listening for any sign of the other man, he suddenly realized that the urge to turn back was not entirely atavistic. *Stop and think*, he told himself.

There was no time for thinking, he wanted to believe. Any hesitation would let his man get across the field, into the heavy brush on the far side. Once given that much head start, a man could run or walk swiftly, cutting north. Rush thought he remembered distant lights on the road, probably one of the small farms that dotted this area. Getting that far, the man could steal or even borrow a ride . . . be swallowed up. He had to be headed off.

Rush listened again to the vast silence.

He decided he was getting nowhere; he had to risk it.

Bracing himself, he got to his hands and knees, then raised himself up to his feet. Slowly he stood, his head poking into the cool, wet layer of night fog rapidly gathering over the field.

The rows of corn stretched straight away from him toward the distant wooded hill. To the right, the rows became indistinct as he looked at them across angles, but a hundred yards away was the weedy black line of a creek or fence row. To the left, the field sloped downhill slightly to another line of high brush, and beyond that the field appeared to be broken by gullies and choked with high weeds.

Slowly Rush turned all the way around, looking for any movement. There was none. It was as if he were alone in the universe, the only sign of life being the two cars at the edge of the deserted road. The Ford still smoked, although the fire had somehow extinguished itself. His Chevrolet sat slightly sideways on the shoulder where he had leaped from it.

His feet were sinking slowly into the rich black gumbo earth. His sweat began to cool, chilling him further. He gritted his teeth and forced himself to remain still, vulnerable. He would see any movement, and this was his only remaining chance.

A long minute ticked off, then another.

Possibly, he told himself, it made little difference. The ones in custody could be induced to talk. There was no reason now for Jane Clarken to maintain her silence. She had to tell her part in this if she hoped to clear herself.

But he knew this last was a vain hope, and the taste of the realization was bitter. She didn't have to talk. She didn't have to admit anything. All they could prove, if he chose to make sure they understood it, was that she had registered under a false name. She had only to say that she had been adventuring. It was hardly the first time a married woman had gone somewhere, used a false name, met another man.

Rush took a deep breath. He was wasting his time, and now he had to face that fact. He turned back toward the road and the cars.

Something erupted into movement in the ditch near the Ford. Something—a man's form—darted between the two automobiles; he heard the sound of gravel being kicked sharp in the deep quiet. Rush understood the movement and had a fleeting, outraged thought—*the car keys!*—and then he ran forward, shouting.

The figure vanished into the front seat of the Chevvie. The door slammed. Rush shouted again, drew up and snapped off a shot. Glass exploded. The Chevvie car engine roared. With the sharp odor of cordite in his nostrils, Rush fired again, aiming for the windshield. The revolver bucked in his hand and more glass flew.

The wheels of the Chevrolet cranked around hard, tires screaming. The engine blatted, misfiring, but then it caught. The car wheeled around the back end of the crippled Ford and fishtailed onto the pavement. Rush, more in frustrated anger than hope, fired again, then once more as the sedan accelerated wildly past the Ford, heading north.

A half-mile up the road the lights flicked on. The car vanished into a dip in the highway, appeared again beyond, and then was gone.

Shaking with disgust, Rush climbed through the broken fence and up to the shoulder of the road. Hot exhaust fumes were settling into the cool layer of ground fog, and the distant hum of the Chevrolet's engine vanished.

Rush leaned against the crumpled fender of the Ford and let the shaking run its course. After a while he turned on the car's emergency flashers. A pickup truck went past without slowing, the driver's face a momentary pale oval through the windshield. Then, in another five minutes, Barry Timmerman and the sheriff came up the side road, flashers going.

Ten

THE morning was clear and hot. There were excited rumors among small groups of people in the lobby and at poolside of Kenton's Run, but the semi-official word from the hotel's management was that someone had been drunk, there had been a slight altercation, but everything was now normal again. The Jenson meetings began again at 9 A.M., on schedule. Children splashed in the pool. Golfers appeared, the sailboats went out, and there was tennis.

Milo Rush met with Barry Timmerman in the coffee shop. Les Montgomery, who had arrived by the time Rush was returned to the lodge, solemnly sat in.

"Your car was found abandoned in Lancaster," Timmerman said. He was drawn and puffy-eyed from lack of sleep. "Naturally there was no sign of the man who drove it."

"He's out of the state by now," Rush concluded glumly.

"Well, there were several other cars stolen in Lancaster last night. Any of them could have taken him to the airport or anywhere else he wanted to go."

"Have the ones in jail said anything at all yet?"

"I talked to the sheriff's office just a few minutes ago. They're stonewalling it."

"What about Mrs. Hendrix?"

Timmerman's lips turned down. "You mean Mrs. Clarken."

"All right. What about her? Will she be charged?"

"As far as I can tell, she's still just a guest here. We'll question her again. Nobody has said out loud that there's any relationship between her and Moradian and the attempted burglary."

"Do you think there's a connection?" Rush asked.

"What I think doesn't matter, Mr. Rush."

Les Montgomery stirred. "How come, man? I mean, you're the chief security officer. I hear you saying they ain't about to pay any attention to you, and that doesn't make much sense."

Timmerman looked into the distance. "The prevailing official theory this morning," he said slowly, "seems to be that none of this would have happened if I had been on the job."

"Well, goddamn, man! You headed 'em off at the pass!"

Timmerman's smile was faint. "It happened, though."

Rush understood. "Scapegoat time?"

"It looks that way."

"Does Jenson operate that way?"

Timmerman's eyes looked like lead. "Jenson operates the way any successful company operates. The good of the corporate image comes first. As far as anyone can determine, there were no photos made of the plans and specifications of the engine layout. The fact remains that people were in the room—twice—and they almost got away. Win Jenson was already saying last night that I should have arranged some kind of a vault for the portfolio case, even if it had to be trucked in from Cincinnati."

"There was the hotel safe."

"Not big enough for those oversize schematics without bending them all up. It was discussed, and I recommended the locked portfolio case. I made a misjudgment. I've already been reminded of that this morning."

The sour flatness of Timmerman's tone was enough to prove that he was having a very bad time. Rush assumed he would lose his job. He felt sorry for Timmerman; he was young enough, perhaps, never to have lost a job before.

"What charges are being filed against the men who were caught?"

"That's all up in the air."

"What do you mean?"

"Nothing has been decided yet. The prosecuting attorney is coming out after a while to talk to Mr. Jenson."

"What are you recommending?"

"Sir, I am no longer in a position to recommend anything to anybody."

Rush decided to give up on that line. "Tell me about the ones who were caught."

"Okay." Timmerman consulted his battered notebook. "Daugherty, J. D. White male. Fifty-one. Six feet. Weight, two thirty-two. Place of birth, Indianapolis. Prior convictions: burglary, second degree, Miami, 1956; assault, Baltimore, 1962. Mechanic several years, various places. Private detective, 1967–70, New Orleans; prior record was found out, he lost his license and got ninety days for false application to the city. Since then, truckdriver, part-time repairman for a camera store in Fort Wayne. Not married.

"Collins, Harvey LeRoy. White male. Thirty-six. Six feet one. One-ninety. Place of birth, San Francisco. No prior record. Army veteran, intelligence school, special training at Fort Benning. FBI school. Field agent, 1966–68. Private investigator since that time except for seven months in 1971 when he worked for Lockheed. Routine plant-guarding job. Married, one kid aged ten, owns an equity in a home in St. Louis, where his wife and kid are right now.

"Schmidt, Burl A. Forty. Five feet eleven. One-sixty. Place of birth, New York City. No prior record. Marines, FBI school, special extra training at the Academy in 1966, detached duty with CIA operation, undesignated, classified, 1968. Released November 1969. No steady employment since that time. School guard. City bus driver. Rejected by the city police in Burlington last year because of his age and a spot on his left lung. Divorced. Present address is in Detroit."

Timmerman closed the book.

Les Montgomery puffed out his cheeks. "Stud crew, huh?"

"They got caught," Rush reminded him.

"They know how to keep quiet," Timmerman added. "No one has gotten anything out of them."

"Not about the other man, either?"

"They say there was no other man."

"And I suppose it would be too much to ask, but nothing has come of circulating the other man's description?"

Timmerman looked uncomfortable. "Well, that's another story."

"What do you mean by that?" Rush demanded.

"Well, the issuance of data has been . . . held up."

"What the hell does *that* mean?"

Timmerman's eyes were goaded and angry. "No official information of any kind has been put out on any of this. The company asked that it be handled this way. To avoid unfavorable publicity."

Rush shoved his chair back abruptly, spilling coffee into his saucer. "Jesus H. Christ."

"The local authorities are cooperating with the company. They don't have much choice about that. They're like everybody else, a little in awe of a big, powerful firm. They want Jenson to use Kenton's Run again, or they hope for other industrial conferences—"

"So they let one of these people get off absolutely free," Rush snapped. "For the sake of their image."

Timmerman watched him but said nothing.

Rush breathed deeply. "All right. Christ. I should know better. I don't know why it should surprise me."

The information hurt, however. Now there was just no hope at all of getting the remaining man. The narrow escape on the roof, the car chase, the comedy of errors in the cornfield—all had been a waste of time.

Unless he could get the identification some other way.

Montgomery said, "What are you thinking, bubba?"

Rush asked Timmerman, "What are my chances of seeing Win Jenson right away?"

Timmerman glanced at his watch. "I'd say they're excellent, because he sent word a while ago that he wanted to talk to you either at the ten-thirty break or at lunchtime."

"Good. That just leaves me time to do something else first. Now tell me this: Will you get Les, here, in to talk to either Collins or Schmidt?"

Timmerman was startled. "In the jail?"

"Yes."

"When?"

"As soon as Les can get to town."

"What excuse can I give them? They won't just let anybody—"

"Les is one of your associates," Rush suggested, curbing impatience.

"I don't know if I should do that."

"You probably don't know what you should do, Barry. But I'm asking you. From what you've already said, I don't really see how your job could be in much more jeopardy than it is already."

Timmerman flushed. "Granted."

"Then get Les in."

"I don't know if it's possible."

"You already said the company is running the show. All it would take is a telephone call."

Timmerman frowned and hesitated.

"Unless," Rush said, "you want to ask Win Jenson's permission first."

Timmerman reddened. "I'll see what I can do."

Rush pushed his chair away from the table. "Les and I will be out by the pool somewhere. We have some things to talk about. Will you let us know right away?"

Timmerman paused again, and Rush felt bad about pushing him so hard. The man was almost dazed by the prospect—more than faint—of losing his job. But Rush had no choice. There were only two or three angles left open to attack. If they all stood pat now, the answers to the planning of the burglary, and—most important to Rush—the story behind Jane Clarken's motivation, might never be uncovered. He had to know this. His stomach seethed with the need to know this.

He let the silence drag out.

"I'll call them," Timmerman said finally.

"Good," Rush said, and took Montgomery out of the coffee shop.

Judith Evans was in one of the groups of women beside the pool, and her expression when Rush walked out showed that she wanted to talk to him. He nodded and went to the far side with Les Montgomery, and quickly filled him in on what to do in Terrydale. Montgomery had figured most of it out for himself, and the conference didn't take long. By the time a waiter came over to see if they wanted anything, Montgomery was ready to go.

"I'll call you," Montgomery said, standing.

"Come back with it," Rush said, "whether you have anything or not. I assume there aren't any more bugs on telephones around here, but let's stay close to the vest for once in this thing."

Montgomery nodded and left.

Rush ordered a glass of milk. Judith Evans detached herself from her friends and walked around the pool. She looked pale beneath her tan, and her swimsuit showed she had not been in the water yet. She walked a trifle self-consciously, barefooted, carrying her towel over her arm. She was walking with control, Rush saw, because her hips would have swayed if she had relaxed, and she did not want that. He felt a little sorry for her.

Her smile against the sun-glare was uncertain. "Good morning."

"Good morning. Will you join me?"

"Do you want me to, or are you being polite?"

"For the lady who saved me from a night trussed up in a bathtub, you're awfully formal. Of course I want you to."

She relaxed and sat across the oval table from him. "Are you all right this morning?"

"I'm fine. You?"

She sighed, her fine breasts moving under the deep cleavage of the suit. "There wasn't much sleep last night."

"Is your husband all right?"

"He's in the meeting."

"That wasn't what I asked."

"I think he's all right, yes."

"He almost lost his engine, you know."

"He was . . . shocked."

"I think a lot of people were shocked. Do you think this might cause them to hurry up on their development program?"

She looked faintly surprised. "I don't know. I hadn't thought of that. Yesterday they decided—"

"You told me that earlier, remember? When I got back last

night and you were both still up. But the burglary attempt might change things."

"Stan didn't say anything about suggesting reconsideration."

Rush shrugged. "It was just a thought."

"Have you seen your—seen Mrs. Hendrix today?"

"No."

"Is she still here?"

"Yes, I think she is."

"You did know her right from the start, didn't you?"

Rush thought about it a moment. "Yes."

Judith Evans leaned back, her face changing. "I won't ask."

"I think I might tell you, a little later."

"Will you?"

"Yes. I might."

"We leave this evening."

"You aren't staying until tomorrow? I thought—"

"I think most of the board will leave tonight. This changed things."

"Nothing was really lost. There hasn't been any publicity."

"I know. But it still changed things. It took all the fun away." Her face twisted briefly. "For those who were having fun."

"What will you and your husband do now?"

"He has a few weeks in the office. Then . . . I don't know yet."

"Do you have any children?"

"No. No children, no grandchildren. It's funny, isn't it? Now we're supposed to sit on the patio of our home and enjoy 'the golden years.' Goddamn that terminology."

"You're too young for that terminology."

Her breath caught. "Am I?"

"You know you are."

"Sometimes I don't know at all."

A young man in a dark business suit left the lobby and walked across to the table. He looked tense and uncomfortable, trying so hard to be brisk. "Mr. Rush?"

"Yes."

"Mr. Jensen could speak with you now, sir."

Rush turned to Judith. "We'll talk a little later today, all right?"

"Yes," she said, her eyes luminous.

Rush went with the boy.

Joe Graeber stood at the window of his hotel room near Broad and High streets in Columbus. The room, except for the wrappings from the new clothes he had bought and the newspaper-wrapped package of mud-soaked clothing, was barren. He had had two hours' sleep in the past forty-eight and he was nearly beside himself.

They were turning on him, he thought. Their refusal to answer his telephone calls proved it. If they didn't reply soon, it could mean not only that they were turning on him, but that they might betray him directly. The waiting was driving him crazy.

Graeber lit one cigarette from another, stared down at the Columbus traffic, and then paced back and forth in the small room.

He was not worried about Schmidt and Collins. Not yet. They were pros. They would keep quiet and they would not panic. The possibility of discovery had been carefully covered along with all other contingencies, and they knew the odds. Sufficient payment had already been made to cover the possibility of a jail term, as unlikely as that might be. The worst they could do, anyway, was provide Graeber's name. They knew nothing more.

Daugherty knew even less. Graeber had no concern about him. Daugherty had been a lamb from the start, and Graeber had made all contacts through two intermediaries, neither of whom knew what was actually going on; they only passed briefcases containing instructions and payments. Even if Daugherty wished to do so, he could not directly involve Graeber. Daugherty had not even known about Schmidt and Collins.

It was the proper way to work. No one knew anyone else. Everything was done through blank contacts. This protected each higher link in the chain if something went wrong. Daugherty knew no one. Schmidt and Collins could only implicate Graeber, at worst, and that was so unlikely it was almost impossible. Graeber himself had been contacted indirectly. All he had was the telephone number and the memory of contacts with two bag men who, even if tracked down, would probably lead him nowhere.

Somehow, Graeber thought furiously, the system had broken down. It was not conceivable to him that any kind of luck had entered into the sudden discovery at Kenton's Run. Everything had gone too well. Jane Clarken had scored with Jack Moradian as planned, and had him off the scene. Daugherty, as expected, had botched his entry and created a disturbance. The backup plan—always the primary plan in Graeber's mind—had begun smoothly. They had needed only about four minutes.

Yet the lawyer, Rush, and some of the others had moved in as if they knew precisely every angle of the plan. *How?*

Graeber could not figure it out. At the moment, the puzzle nagged at him yet seemed secondary. He had to know what his superiors were doing now . . . how he was supposed to proceed. The telephone call was vital.

When the room telephone did finally ring, it startled him so that he dropped his cigarette. Retrieving it hurriedly from the shag carpet, he reflected that he had to take a pill soon and rest. The car chase and hair's-breadth escape in the field, coupled with the car theft in Lancaster and later path-covering actions in Columbus, had chewed up his nerves.

But the telephone call could only be one person. He grabbed up the instrument anxiously. "Yeah?"

"Joe?" The soft, weak-sounding male voice was familiar.

"Yes. Right. Listen—"

"We'll be brief, Joe. We know what took place."

So somebody at the other end had made contact, too, Graeber thought. "All right. What happens now?"

"We sit tight," the voice told him. For some reason he thought the voice belonged to a lawyer somewhere. "There haven't been any filings."

"Are you going to see to it that they get some legal—"

"That was part of the bargain. If it comes to that, yes."

"All right. What am I supposed to do?"

"Nothing," the voice said.

"Forget it?" Graeber said, surprised.

"That's correct."

"What about the others?"

"I told you—"

"They're going to be taken care of?"

"If that becomes necessary, yes."

"I just forget it?"

"That is correct."

Graeber took a ragged breath. "I need some money."

"Money?"

"I lost every bit of equipment down there. I've got about enough left to pay my bill here and get a plane ticket. That's all."

There was a muffled pause, and Graeber got the impression the man on the other end was talking with someone else. Then the voice came back. "You were paid all necessary expenses and a retainer."

"That's right," Graeber bit off. "But I gave almost all of it to the others. Dau—uh, one of them had to have his full payment in advance. It was the only way he would deal. And the others had to be given part of their share. I gave them just about all I had, to make sure of a good job. And some of that equipment wasn't cheap. We had car rentals, travel, all the rest."

"There won't be any further payment."

"*What?* Look, I don't expect anything like the full amount. Hell's bells. We didn't deliver. But you can't just leave me out in the cold! What about my expenses? What about getting myself away from here, set up again?"

The voice was calm, bloodless. "The others will be dealt with as necessary. No further action by you is necessary under any circumstances. The client sees no reason to send good money after bad. What's already been expended must simply be written off as a bad investment. I suggest you go home and forget it."

"*Negative*, you son of a bitch! The deal was clear enough! I've got at least ten grand more coming, even the way things turned out! If you think you can get away with something less, you're dead wrong!"

"Forget it, Joe."

There was a click.

Stunned, Graeber stood holding a dead telephone.

"Hello?" he croaked. "*Hello!*" Silence answered him.

He threw the phone against the wall, turned, and knocked the lamp off the table. He kicked it under the bed. They wouldn't get away with it. He would—he would. . . .

He wouldn't do a thing.

There wasn't anything he could do. He knew ways to trace the telephone number. But he also knew he would now find a disconnect, and a neolithic telephone company about as likely to provide information as the Pentagon. Besides, there were probably multiple contacts beyond him, too, and right now he was sure they were already breaking up, covering tracks.

Someone had wanted the engine plans badly. Someone he didn't even know, and now never would know. And without this knowledge, he was helpless.

Scooping up the soggy newspaper parcel of muddy clothes, he hurled them against the wall. The parcel burst and fell to the floor. He kicked the pieces and strode to the window and fired a fresh cigarette. His head felt ready to split.

Cycling, his brain jumped from the capture of the others to the chase to the telephone call to the contacts with Daugherty to the way he had used Jane Clarken. He had felt sure it was under control when he had Schmidt and Collins put Milo Rush out of action for the night. And yet it had been Milo Rush who almost caught him on the roof. How had he gotten loose? How had he known some second attempt would be made?

How had Rush been there in the first place?

Graeber's mind cycled back to Jane Clarken.

The telephone call had sounded as if she were trying to get rid of Rush. That could have been faked. It could have been a trick. She might have guessed about a tap on her line. She was smart . . . too smart. She had always lorded it over him, treated him like dirt.

What, Graeber thought suddenly, if she had been feeding Rush information right from the start?

What if she had been going through all of it only to blow the entire operation as it developed?

Graeber stood up straight as the idea grabbed his vitals in a cold vise. It made a kind of sense. Operations did not often fail because of blind luck. If Jane Clarken, the little whore, had been feeding Milo Rush information—working with him and staying in close contact throughout—then everything was explained. It was Jane who had finally guessed the plan. It was Jane who had gotten Rush freed after Schmidt and Collins put him out of action. It was Jane who had fouled up everything, just as she had been plenty willing to spread it for anybody Graeber had told her to oblige in the old days, but then had refused him, had treated him like scum, making him feel worthless, like a goddamned puppy dog sniffing around her elegant ass while she acted as if he didn't exist. . . .

Yes, it all made sense this way. Graeber's simmering emotions cried out that it was true. She had always acted too good for him, had always given it to anybody else . . . panting, writhing in those hidden films, refusing even to talk to *him* . . . she had acted in the same cool, regal way when he contacted her in Washington, hadn't even thawed when he produced the pictures and made her go along with it . . . treating him that way, as if she hated him . . . and if she had been smart, if she had known how he really felt about her, how he wanted to hold her and give her things and see her eyes change for him. . . .

But the goddamned bitch whore had always been too good, too high and mighty for him, and even now, during this job, she had been setting him up. Maybe she had already told Rush and the police everything, enough to have him picked up, so she could come and laugh at him.

Graeber was frozen by the picture of it.

It made sense.

She had been the one who had blown the entire operation.

But they hadn't caught him, he thought with a sudden spasm of glee. Nor would they. He was free and clear, for now. She would go back home, thinking she had beaten him. But she hadn't won the last round. Not yet. He had figured it out, and that gave him a weapon. He was going to get even, not just for this, not just for the past, not just for the way she always made him feel, but for all of it.

He was going to get her. Once and for all.

Eleven

TWO other men were in the suite with Win Jenson when Milo Rush was ushered in. Jenson, in shirtsleeves and drinking coffee over several typed reports or documents on a low table, gave Rush a weak handshake and introduced the other two by names that meant nothing to Rush. They were contemporaries of Jenson's, probably top officials. They stayed. Everyone sat down in easy chairs around the low table.

"Coffee, Mr. Rush?" Jenson asked.

"Thanks, no."

Jenson leaned forward. "I've been fully filled in on the help you gave in last night's unpleasantness. The firm sincerely appreciates it."

"I hope there was no serious damage," Rush said.

"No, there sure wasn't. Nothing was taken, and from what I can learn, there's no way the man who was on the roof could have gotten any information at all."

"Do you have any idea who he might be?"

"No, afraid not."

"I assume you're trying to find out?"

"I hope to tell you we are. It looks like those punks who were caught aren't going to talk, though. We've instructed our lawyers to enter into bargaining with them in the hope one of them might be willing to trade information for a deal on charges. So far, no good on that."

"What are your ideas on who might be behind the operation?"

"We have no set ideas."

"You must have some suspicions."

Jenson's face drew tight. "Actually, Mr. Rush, I didn't invite you here to talk about any suspicions we might or might not have. You must realize there are areas of confidentiality."

It was the kind of stuffy little speech Rush would have expected from this man, so he was not really surprised. "Sorry."

Jenson immediately turned on his once-boyish smile to make amends. "It could be anyone, you know. I wouldn't want to accuse any of our competitors, large or small. By making a hullabaloo about the attempt, we only would advertise that we have something on the back burner. No sense adding new troubles, right?"

Jenson's aides grinned as if vastly amused by his statement. Rush wondered why he disliked the man so intensely. It went partly to the gutting of Stan Evans, he thought, as well as to personality.

He said, "I've heard there won't be any news about the attempted break-in if you can keep it quiet."

"That kind of publicity is only bad publicity, Mr. Rush. We're fortunate in having chosen a rural area where the local press is not given to excessive snooping. As far as anyone will know, there was a simple room burglary attempt, nothing to do with Jenson. Nothing at all. You see why this is necessary, of course."

"I can see advantages. My concern isn't with Jenson but with finding the man who got away."

Jenson cocked his head. "Do you have some personal interest?"

He was sharper than he acted. "Only the personal interest motivated by being hit on the head and dumped in my own bathtub."

Jenson chuckled at this, so his two aides chuckled too. "Needless to say, sir, the firm also regrets your personal inconvenience. You can be sure we are moving to tighten our own security in the future. We'll have no recurrences."

"I thought," Rush said, "Barry Timmerman did a good job."

Jenson smiled coldly. "There are times when blame must be

placed. Timmerman was responsible. Life is hard. Excuses and last-minute repair jobs are not good enough sometimes. I'm sure that to you Timmerman appeared capable. The fact is that it was a very near thing. The firm cannot tolerate that sort of slipshod work—not on the assembly line, in the labs, in an office, or on a security matter."

"He loses his job, then?"

"That's not your concern, Mr. Rush. In all due respect."

"And Jack Moradian?"

Jenson exchanged irritated glances with his aides. When he turned back to Rush, his face was bland again. "Our primary concern, sir, was your attitude toward filing of charges against the men in custody in Terrydale."

"That's not for me to say, is it?"

"I understand they did attack you, as you mentioned."

"Identification is impossible. They wore masks."

"If the masks are found?"

"Have they been found?"

Jenson's face creased in irritation. "No, sir."

"Then it's academic," Rush pointed out.

"You have no intention of urging that charges be pressed in the attack on your person?"

"I would probably go anything up to the death penalty for the one who hit me with the sap. But I can't make identification."

Jenson leaned back and locked his hands over one knee in a curiously girlish gesture. "A firm such as ours can never afford adverse publicity, Mr. Rush. In this case, any lurid story about an attempted burglary would make the firm look bad. In addition, of course, questions would be raised about what product or process we have that motivated industrial espionage. Jenson wants none of that."

"I fail to see how a story about a burglary is adverse publicity."

"We have a carefully worked out long-range public relations plan. All statements, publicity, speeches, interviews—our paid advertising—all dovetail with our concept of the Jenson image. In our view, any publicity outside the realm of our programmed information is possibly adverse."

"I've run into other companies that always want everything hushed up. It interests me as a theory. How can a story in a newspaper about a burglary hurt your company?"

Jenson waved the question away. "It isn't *favorable* publicity, is it? Therefore, it can't help us. If it can't help us, we want to avoid it."

Rush gave up.

"Our lawyers," Jenson went on, "are of the opinion that any meaningful conviction is unlikely. Oh, the local authorities might possibly get a small sentence for Daugherty, because he has a prior record. The chances appear good that the other two could beat the charges, or win suspended sentences, no matter how vigorously the case might be pursued."

Rush didn't say anything.

"Would you agree with that estimate?" Jenson asked.

"I think it would all depend on the quality of the prosecution and defense, and how strongly your company and the lodge pressed the matter."

Jenson showed even white teeth. "Spoken like a true lawyer. But perhaps you don't know, sir, that Kenton's Run is by no means eager to press the matter."

"Bad publicity?"

"If you operated a hotel of this type, would you enjoy seeing stories that revealed guests might be burglarized?"

Rush got it. "And Jenson isn't anxious to press the charges either."

"We intend to hold out the rest of the day, if we can, with the impression we want maximum effort made. We still have a faint hope one of those men might talk and reveal his sources. *That's* what we're really interested in, not penny-ante prosecution."

Rush had to smile. "So the three in jail probably won't be charged—or at least the charges, if filed, won't be prosecuted—because neither you nor the hotel will testify."

"We simply don't see justice, or our own ends, being served . . . if we actively press the matter."

"So they'll go free, and the only ones who lose in the long run will be Timmerman and probably Moradian."

"Those are internal matters."

"I see."

"You won't, ah, strenuously object if charges are not lodged?"

"That's a good pun," Rush said. "I won't object aloud, no. I suspect it would do me very little good."

Jenson exhaled deeply. "We appreciate your consideration in all of this, Mr. Rush. I wonder, since you are an attorney, would you consider some small retainer fee proper? As payment, you might say, for services rendered?"

Rush stood. "Don't worry. Your precious little secret is safe with me."

"I wasn't suggesting a *payoff!* I was offering, in all good faith—"

"Well, forget it."

"Are you always so sensitive, Mr. Rush?"

"It's a problem I've had all my life," Rush said from the door. "I am always repelled by horseshit. Good day, gentlemen."

He closed the door on their startled faces.

Down among the tree houses, the heat of the day had only begun to penetrate the shade. It was very quiet, and off in the distance was the sound of children's voices. Still angry, Rush walked down the gravel path and found the curtains of Jane Clarken's tree house all securely drawn. There was no sign of life within.

He went up onto the narrow redwood porch and rapped on the door. It vibrated, hollow-sounding. There was no response. The wind stirred the pines, making them sway gently in sun-mottled patterns.

Rush tried the door handle. Locked.

He leaned close to the door. "I don't want to kick it in, Jane."

He waited again.

There was a slight sound inside and the door lock clicked. Jane opened the door. She wore no makeup, and circles under her eyes showed lack of sleep. She wore a shapeless corduroy robe and was barefooted. She said nothing as she turned from him and walked back to the couch, where she sat down very stiffly, huddling as if against pain.

Rush locked the door behind him. "What have they told you?"

"I can't check out," she said hollowly. She did not look at

him. "They were very polite. They said there might be more questions later, and I should stay."

"There won't be any charges."

Her eyes, large and frightened, swept up to his.

"Yes," he said in reply to the obvious question. "I'm sure."

"Does that mean I can leave now?"

"I'm not an official spokesman. I'm only telling you what I know for a fact. If I were you, I'd expect some official word late today."

She stared again into space. "Jack has been here three times in the last hour, hammering on the door. I didn't answer."

"You'll have to put up with that."

"Don't be sarcastic, Milo. I don't think I can stand any more."

"He's going to lose his job."

"He wasn't part of anything. He didn't know—"

"He was careless," Rush said. "He almost was a party to Jenson's losing its precious whatever-it-is. A skirt-chaser. A womanizer. Weak in the head and too strong in the britches. He's had it."

Jane's lips compressed in a thin line of pain. She kept quiet.

Rush said, "You knew that would happen to him anyway. Why pretend you give a damn . . . about him or anybody else?"

"What do you want, Milo? Did you just come down here to preach at me? I don't need any of that!"

"What do you need?"

She refused to look at him or speak.

"Do you plan to go back home?" he asked. "To Dave?"

"Yes." Then she turned quickly and faced him. "But I suppose a lot of that depends on you now, doesn't it?"

"Meaning?"

"If you choose to tell him the truth about this, what chance do I have of ever making it up?"

"What do you suggest I tell him? That you came down here to play croquet?"

"God*damn* you, Milo! Why are you acting like this? Do you think you can make me feel any worse? *What do you want?*"

"I want to know why. I want to know about the photographs and the man who sent them to you, and why you were furnished money for a new wardrobe and a new identity. I want all of it."

Her eyes, wide with shock, studied his face. "What do you know . . . about the photographs?"

"I know a lot about the photographs."

"How—"

"Because Dave told me about them."

"Dave didn't—"

"The hell he didn't. He was there when the mail came that day."

She collapsed backward on the couch, her head lolling on the backrest. "Oh, God. Oh, no."

"You've got that much to explain to him anyway," Rush said inexorably. "You might as well tell me all of it."

Eyes closed, she shook her head. "No."

"He wanted the plans," Rush told her. "He had the pictures and used them to force you to cooperate. You thought you could hide everything this way. I don't know what you planned to tell poor Dave when you got back. He's gone crazy over this. Maybe you weren't thinking very clearly yourself. You figured you could work it out some way. So you came here, you made sure the right man was intrigued, and you maneuvered it so he was here, rather than in his room, at the time the burglary was set up."

She sat up stiffly again, watching him with haunted eyes.

"Who is he?" Rush asked.

She closed her eyes tight and shook her head.

"He can't hurt you. Not if you tell me."

"No."

"Do you know who he was working for?"

She shook her head again.

"You're not going to help yourself this way," Rush told her.

"Do you think anything is going to help me?"

"Tell me what it was all about. All of it. I can help."

"You can't help."

"What was in your mind?" Rush bored in. "Did you think you could vanish with that kind of a silly story and expect Dave to believe it?"

"I don't know what I thought. I wasn't thinking."

"Didn't you know he'd check on you?"

"I didn't know he had seen those pictures!"

"Do you think he would have believed you anyway?"

"He might have—he would have—if it hadn't been for seeing the pictures."

"And then you would have just gone back home as if nothing had ever happened."

Her voice strained with anger. "I don't know how I would have gone back. I would have gone back. I know that. It would have been all right."

"*How?*"

"We would have . . . been all right."

"You would have kept telling the same lie?"

"Yes. What else could I have done?"

"And gone again if the same man asked you again?"

"No!"

"What makes you think this would have been the end of it?"

"He said it would be. He promised."

Rush was astonished. "And you believed him?"

"Don't you see? With this, I would have had information against *him*, too! He couldn't have forced me to cooperate anymore—I could say I would tell the police if he pressed me any further."

"And implicate yourself in the process."

"I didn't know what was going to be involved here, exactly."

"Did you think it was going to be a picnic?"

"Damn you!"

"Then answer me straight. You knew you were coming here to be bait. You knew it was a blackmail scheme or a burglary or something illegal. Whatever you did for this man earlier was illegal too, wasn't it?"

"It wasn't illegal—"

"Do you want me to explain to you about some of the laws on the books? Prostitution? Sodomy? Pandering? Probable blackmail? Obscenity? Making appointments for immoral purposes? Conspiracy to—"

"*All right!*" Her face twisted. "But that was a long time ago—it's all in the past. I'm sorry for it. I can't live it over again!"

"It looks to me," Rush told her softly, "like you started living it over again last night."

"Oh, damn you, Milo!"

"I don't think you wanted any of this. You've been used. I have no idea what you might try to tell Dave except at least part of the truth."

"I can't tell him that!"

"Let me finish. You tell me who this man is and what it was all about. Everything you know. Then I'll find him. I promise you that. We'll talk about how you can try to patch it up with Dave, you and I. It isn't going to be easy, but you have a chance."

"I don't know if there is any chance now."

"There's almost always a chance. If you want it."

"You know I want it."

"Then tell me the whole story so I can try to help."

She stared at him, her eyes tortured. "It will only make things worse. There's nothing you or anybody else can do."

Rush was running out of patience. This was all painful for him, too. He forced himself to go on, pressing her. "Did he promise he'd give you the negatives if you did this?"

"Yes." Her head was down.

"Didn't it occur to you to come to me then and tell the whole thing? Wouldn't that have made more sense? Didn't it occur to you that he could duplicate negatives, too? Don't you realize that your whole pattern of behavior was crazy, expecting Dave to believe that transparent story—"

"I'm sorry I didn't think clearly," she said with savage sarcasm. "It's very easy for someone to sit back and coolly say what another person should have done. I was half out of my mind, and I'm afraid of him, and I did the only thing I could think of."

"And the next time, if you get out of this with a marriage, you'll do what he says again."

"No. No. This is *it*."

"It won't be over until you tell me everything. That's the only way we can make *sure* of putting an end to it."

She began to cry. "It's hopeless. I've been a damned fool all my life. But"—she hesitated—"all right. I'll tell you."

When Milo Rush left the tree house an hour later, puffy gray clouds had begun to gather overhead, and there was a sultry promise of rain. He walked slowly through the woods to the tennis courts, past the cabana and into the lobby of Kenton's Run. He was profoundly depressed. People pretended to themselves that they were logical. They invented all manner of excuses for their actions, erected frameworks of stated beliefs and often said they were willing to fight for them. But then, at the most crucial moments, they became what they really were: baffled, uncertain, illogical creatures driven by instinct and blind chance.

Jane Clarken's story had not really surprised him. He should have guessed the parts he had not known. And yet, despite his own best judgment, revelations of stupidity, greed and fear almost always did shake him at some deep, unsuspected level. He wondered if he would ever learn.

Of course he had shown none of his reactions. He was supposed to be the strong one, right?

The strong one. The irony of it swept over him. Jane Clarken was depending on him now. And back in Washington, poor dumb, uninformed, trusting Dave was counting on him too. There was no way things could be repaired. Not by him and not even by them. They had to face each other, and the truth . . . or at least much of the truth. And then they would do what people always did in such times. They would face it, and see how they reacted, and in the process try to understand the people they had become. No one could predict the outcome, if there ever were outcomes.

As the air conditioning settled coolly around him, he thought of the other things that had yet to be done. They depressed him, too.

By lunchtime Les Montgomery was back from Terrydale. The hotel was crowded and busy with vacationers and noon-breaking conventioneers wolfing down prefab meals. Rush took Montgomery to his room.

"You talked to them?" Rush asked when the door was closed.

"Yeah, man," Montgomery said, stretching across the bed. "Old Barry was right, though. They're really stonewalling it."

"They wouldn't tell you anything?"

"Man, they wouldn't gimme the time of day."

"Did you get them separately?"

"Hubba hubba. For all the good it did me."

"What does the sheriff say?"

"He is pissed, man. He's got word from the district attorney that they might not file."

Rush accepted the news without comment. It had been a faint hope anyway.

"I did a little better on the other deal, though," Montgomery said.

"How so?"

"Well, I called Rutherford in New York, and he knew what I was talking about right away when I mentioned Jenson stock."

Rush waited, getting himself set inside for this news, which was also not unexpected.

"It's a pretty tightly held company," Montgomery told him. "So that's why he noticed about three, four months ago when itty-bitty pieces of the stock started coming on the market. He says he just happened to notice because the stuff is out so infrequently. The Jenson stock just started appearing in dabs, a hundred shares offered here, a hundred there."

"About how much changed hands? Any idea?"

"He couldn't be exact, but he thinks probably about a thousand shares, all told."

"And Jenson is selling for what?"

"About one-ten now. It was inching up after *The Wall Street Journal* had that story, and that was another reason Rutherford thought it was weird, stock appearing for sale when it was getting more valuable. He says it sold for about a hundred, most of it. Gobbled right up."

"Had he heard about any other queries on the transactions?"

"Nope. Of course he probably wouldn't, if it was discreet. He says little pieces of the stock are going around now since the rise in value, but officers in the company and all still probably hold over ninety percent of it. I guess nobody got very curious except us."

Rush rubbed the back of his neck where the headache was building. "Any word on the seller?"

Montgomery frowned. "He knows a man who knows a man, and he had a guess."

"Who is he guessing?"

"Just who you think it is, bubba."

"That's just great."

"You know, it occurs to me that we been dealing with some real stupid people here."

"No. Just people."

Montgomery made a face. "Look at Jane. Why in the *hell* did she get herself messed up in this? And the more you look, the more folks you find that have just flat screwed themselves all up when there ought to have been a cooler way to handle things."

"If you want to sit back and sneer from the bleachers, you're in the wrong business, Les. You take people the way they really are in this line of work: muddled, confused, under pressure, not thinking straight."

"It don't do much for your faith in your fellow man, bubba."

"No," Rush agreed. "But it sure teaches you to live with what *is*, rather than what should be."

Twelve

BY the middle of the afternoon, dense rain clouds had turned the Ohio sky gloomy gray. An electric humidity hung over the hills. The rain had not yet begun, however, and the poolside patio was crowded with those getting its maximum benefit before the storm broke.

With Les Montgomery already headed back for Washington, Milo Rush had gone through a series of brief meetings to begin to wind things up at Kenton's Run; he would check out with Jane Clarken before 6 P.M., he had assured the desk, and the sheriff had assured him there would be no problem with her departure. Lacking a complaint from either Jenson or the lodge, the sheriff was going to press for a misdemeanor case of disturbing the peace against Daugherty, Schmidt and Collins, but he admitted sourly that he was only doing this to make a record, and in the hope they would plead guilty, pay a fine and be on their way. The sheriff had some bitter words about people who would not help the law prosecute offenders. Rush did not bother to try to console him, except to point out that it happened all the time. The sheriff was not the type to understand concerns about "bad publicity."

Rush waited in the lobby for the afternoon coffee break in the Jenson meetings with a feeling of sourness not unlike the sheriff's. He was not given to undue concern about the conservatives' cries for stronger law and order, but he was struck with a certain sense of irony. Joe Graeber, the man whose name he had finally gotten from Jane, was out of this clean. The three men who had worked with him would be free with, at worst, a meaningless misdemeanor count against them. Jane was the one who would suffer. And Dave. And the man Rush was now waiting to spot and talk with.

When Rush finally did locate him, it was a slight surprise, because Stanley Evans was not in some group of executives balancing coffee cups in the lower corridor, or huddled over documents in the crowded coffee shop, but at poolside.

He was at one of the canopy tables set well back from the pool. He was alone and had just ordered a drink from one of the white-coated waiters. He had removed his dark gray suit coat and draped it over an empty chair, and his tie was pulled down, his collar opened. As usual he was smoking fiercely, although his attitude was slumped, exhausted.

The impression of exhaustion became much sharper as Rush approached him. Although Evans had earlier appeared worn out, with an inner malaise that somehow defied description, he was much worse today. His pallor was striking, and his cheeks were sunken as if in death. When he saw Rush, he failed dismally in an obvious effort to rouse himself and appear more convivial.

"I ordered a martini, Mr. Rush. You'll join me?"

"Thanks. Maybe later. You have time for a drink before you have to get back inside?"

Evans watched the pool play with his dead eyes. "Oh, yes. I have lots of time."

"How long is the break?"

"It doesn't really matter. I'm through for the day."

Rush was not much surprised. "I had the impression you wouldn't be winding up your duties for a little while yet."

"Well, that's been . . . moved up."

"Have you told your wife yet?"

"No, it's, uh, just developed. I'm sure she'll be delighted." Evans made an attempt to buck himself up and grin, and the effect was ghastly. "Now we can begin our retirement program at once, y' see."

Rush looked around the pool area.

"She's in the room, I think," Evans said.

"Do you intend to tell her about it?"

"Of course. As I said, she'll be delighted. We plan—"

"I don't mean about immediate retirement."

"What do you mean, then?"

Rush ignored the gambit. "Are they going to file criminal charges against you, Mr. Evans?"

Looking very old, Evans lighted one cigarette from another. His hands shook. "No. . . . So you know about it."

"Most of it."

"Win Jenson told you? He said—"

"For once, he might have told you the truth. At least he said nothing to me."

"How do you know, then?"

"There hasn't been any leak," Rush assured him. "I assume not even the other members of the board know."

"But *you* know. How?"

"The stock sales."

Evans's face twisted in pain. "That's how Win found out, too. Although the utmost discretion was used."

"It isn't that easy to unload a hundred thousand dollars' worth of stock in a company as closely held as this one."

Evans sighed and said nothing.

"How did you happen to contact Joe Graeber?" Rush asked.

Evans looked at him. "Who?"

"Graeber. The man in charge of the attempted operation last night."

"Oh. I didn't even know his name. I went through . . . intermediaries."

"Did you know they would use burglary?"

"I won't pretend with you, Mr. Rush. May I say to you, sir, that I consider you, as of this moment, potential counsel."

"I have no intention of letting any of this go any further. Client-counsel privilege has nothing to do with it."

"Still, sir, if charges were later to be filed—"

"In that case I'll promise confidentiality."

Evans's shoulders slumped further. "I didn't know what means might be used. I didn't want to know."

"Your instructions were to get copies of the engine designs?"

"Only a very small part is vital. Designs for the cylinder heads are the crucial matter. That's all I cared about."

"Did you plan to sell them to someone else?"

Evans looked sincerely surprised. "If the plans had been stolen, my program for accelerated development would have been vindicated, don't y' see."

"I don't see," Rush admitted.

"Win has downgraded this project from its inception. If the program had been developed by anyone else . . . anyone at all in the firm . . . it would have been given much higher priority. Jenson-designed engines would be projected for models to be introduced later this year. But it was *my* project, don't y' see. So it had to be downgraded . . . slowed and held up. It couldn't be brought to fulfillment until after I had left the board. It had to appear to be Win's personal project when it finally came out. Under the guises of orderly development, caution, extra engineering study—anything else he could throw up as a routine roadblock—it was held up month after month, even year after year. I fought for every cent that went into R and D for this item. In every meeting, in every memo, he had new questions and new problems. Finally when I began to make it a major issue, for the good of the firm, he began bringing in bogus reports to make the whole project look silly, too visionary." Evans's hands trembled more violently.

"You fought him," Rush said.

"I did." Evans smiled, but again it was like a death mask. "This is one of those companies, sir, where middle management talks about saving the firm from its ownership. I knew Win's father. He started with nothing and built a fine company. He killed himself doing it. Win took control at a time when he was much more interested in his polo ponies and jet-set girlfriends. Later he made the firm his main toy—after I had put in *more* years, running it for him in his virtual absence. And then, when I knew we had this configuration that could revolutionize motor-car manufacture, put Jenson at the center of a vast new arm of the industry—" Evans paused, inhaled deeply, and coughed. His eyes watered and he reached for the drink that the waiter had just put in front of him. He sipped it, blinking bright-eyed, obviously shaken.

"Has your fall from grace been entirely because of this engine plan?" Rush asked.

"No," Evans said, and managed to invest the single word with corrosive bitterness. "I've been around too long for Win. There are those who feel they owe me . . . loyalty. People seek my opinion on policy matters. There was a time when my word in the board room meant almost automatic voting in whatever direction I suggested. He had to break that up, don't y' see, if it was to be wholly *his* company."

"But it *is* his company," Rush reminded him gently.

Evans stared into space. "Yes."

"Did you really think loss of the plans would change events?"

"It would have. Theft would have been a shock. It would have shown the other board members the extent of what we have here. I could have spoken up for accelerated development . . . again. They would have listened. They would have voted with *me* again, instead of with Win."

"And if that failed, you had the plans to take elsewhere."

"I don't like to think of that as a viable alternative, Mr. Rush."

Their eyes met, and Rush decided to let the point go. It was already answered.

Evans seemed to sense this. "I've given my life to Jenson, Mr. Rush. I do not think I ever believed it would be necessary to take my plan somewhere else."

Rush didn't say anything.

Evans added, "After what I've given to this company, I had something coming—either vindication, or the right to go elsewhere with something that was mine, something I had fought for . . . killed myself for."

It was an eerie kind of afterthought. It was not, Rush sensed, wholly a figure of speech. He wondered what kind of medical report lay in a doctor's files somewhere on Stanley Evans. Progressive heart disease? Cancer? What kind of medical pronouncement of doom, atop the savage beatings in endless meetings and memos and confrontations, drove a man to risk everything remaining to him on a wild scheme which at best could never have had more than a marginal chance?

"You can't understand," Evans said, "how much I've given to this company."

"I suppose I can't," Rush said wearily. "And what happens now?"

Evans raised an eyebrow. "Ah, well. That is a very good question, Mr. Rush. Naturally, Win will do everything in his power to strip me of pension and other benefits."

"You might fight that."

"And have him bring out in the open everything he knows? Hardly."

"The stocks you sold aren't your total worth."

"Very nearly. We've always lived well, don't y' see. Oh, our home is paid for. There are a few stocks left. We can go on as long as I . . . as long as might be necessary."

Rush felt a sense of enormous defeat. "The hundred thousand was mostly used up?"

"Well over half. A remainder is with an attorney. He isn't a very ethical attorney. I rather doubt my chances of getting any of it back at this stage."

"You've taken a hell of a beating. For an engine."

"It wasn't the engine. Oh, I had pride in it. I've always believed that the man who doesn't love his work is a man who isn't alive. I've always invested everything in my work. I've always given myself to it. I loved that engine. I loved the plan. I wanted to see it come out right. I wanted to be a part of it. I wanted them to see I'm not that old and used up quite yet; I still have a little left. But it wasn't the engine, really. It was loving the company, you see . . . loving my own part in it, wanting my . . . wanting what I had coming, don't you see."

At the doors to the lobby, Judith Evans appeared. She was in her swimsuit. She saw them, smiled, waved, started toward them.

"What will you tell her?" Rush asked.

"I don't know. Some of it. Not all. I have to tell her some."

"Yes."

"I want to tell her in my own way, Mr. Rush. At my own time."

"Yes. I understand that."

"The hardest part will be telling her the things we can't do. God, I hate telling her that!"

Evans's voice rose slightly with the last words, showing the force of pain still alive inside him. But his wife was quite near the table by now, really a very pretty woman, smiling at them, carrying her beach towel over a sun-pinkened shoulder. His expression did not betray his feelings, and as she reached their table he looked milky-eyed, passive.

"So there the two of you are!" she said. "Don't either of you plan to do any work this afternoon?"

"We decided to rest," Rush told her after it became apparent Evans was not going to speak.

"Could I persuade either of you to find a swimsuit and join me in the water before the rain comes?"

Evans again chain-lighted cigarettes. "I'm content, my dear."

"Are you going back to the meetings? It looked like they were starting again."

"No. I thought I'd sit this one out and take the sun."

Judith Evans frowned at the sky, then at her husband. "But there isn't any sun, darling."

"You're right." Evans smiled. "But the air is pleasant, isn't it?"

Judith stared at him for a moment, as if quietly baffled. Then her determined smile returned and she looked at Rush. "How about you, Milo? A swim?"

Before he could answer, there was a scurrying around the pool, people beginning to climb out, and heavy raindrops began spattering down on the pavement around them, making little geysers in the pool water.

"Damn!" Judith said in exasperation.

Evans gathered up cigarettes and lighter. "Just as well. Shall we get inside, dear?"

Everyone was running for cover.

"I suppose so," Judith said with a little frown. "What can we do? Shall we try the bar, the three of us? I can change in a minute."

"Let's let Mr. Rush pursue his own activities," Evans said easily. "If you don't mind, there are a few things you and I ought to talk about."

She looked at him. Perhaps she sensed something in his manner. Perhaps there had been so much bad news lately that she automatically assumed this would be bad, too.

"If you like, darling," she said somberly.

Evans stood, picked up his coat, put his arm around her. "Excuse us, Mr. Rush?"

Judith smiled. "We'll have that drink a little later today. Right?"

"Right," Rush said, making his facial muscles smile.

He watched them hurrying across the patio in the gathering rain, the nice woman with a body that was still young and good, and the very old-appearing man. The rain pounded down into the empty blue pool, to be absorbed and diluted and chlorinated and filtered and recycled and, like so many other things, ultimately wasted.

Thirteen

ALTHOUGH Marty had gone to Milo Rush's home for feeding chores as usual while he was away from Washington, his extensive collection of tropical fish showed definite signs of mild hysteria when he began turning on tank lights not long after dawn Saturday. To be on the safe side, his instructions to Marty were for drastic underfeeding, and the fish were ravenous. Still in his robe, he was standing beside a 150-gallon aquarium, watching the oscars tear up chunks of beef heart, when the telephone rang.

He picked up the extension in the paneled hallway between the main fish room and the study.

"Milo?" It was Dave Clarken and he was upset. "When did you get back? Why didn't you call me? Is Jane with you?"

"We had some weather and we didn't get in until two this morning," Rush said, popping the patty of frozen beef heart up and down in his left hand to avoid freezing his fingers. "I decided it was a little late, and everybody was too tired."

"Is Jane—"

"She's with me, Dave. I brought her here. She's all right."

"I want to talk to her right now. Nobody has told me anything that makes sense. Montgomery convinced me to cool it until today, but I've had it, Milo. I want some answers. If you think I'm going to buy that business trip story, or—"

"She's asleep upstairs in the guest room, Dave. Where are you?"

"I'm at home. I've *been* at home. Damn it—"

"Why don't you come on over here?"

"I'll be there in thirty minutes."

Rush replaced the telephone. His watch showed 7 A.M. He had the beginnings of a fresh headache. It felt discouragingly like the old one. Barefooted, he padded back into the fish room and finished turning on tank lights. The paneled addition to the mansion was carpeted, had a fireplace, and was furnished with leather couches and chairs as well as outlets for his stereo system. But its main function was a place for his hobby, which continually threatened to get out of hand. In addition to the oscar tank, one wall was almost entirely devoted to other aquariums, most of the twenties and thirties arranged behind sliding panels for easy access. Flanking the fireplace were two 100-gallon tanks, and on the outside wall, arranged with the oscar tank, were a 300-gallon aquarium and a pair of 75-gallon saltwater setups. Rush moved along the paneled wall, feeding his anabantid collection, the African cichlids, the tetras, and the various livebearers. Tinfoil barbs and silver dollars flashed brilliantly as he tended to the hundreds, also checking filtration systems and thermometers. Pausing to inspect his breeder orandas, he moved on to the saltwater apparatus, where he was greeted by the flashing gold and blue of sergeant majors and damsels, the pulse of anemones and the bellicose beauty of an isolated prize lionfish. With the quickness of his expertise, he finished the morning feeding, mentally noted the various jobs he would have to take care of as soon as possible, and returned his food containers to the compact wet room and freezer area that adjoined. He did not turn on the main lights here to check the betas; he was preoccupied.

He walked back through the paneled corridor, past the kitchen area and dining room, went through the foyer and into the large living room, and opened the draperies onto the patio. He stood for a moment looking out over the patio, with its fish pond, and the small swimming pool tucked into the tightly manicured garden beyond. He wondered if there was time for a quick swim. He decided not.

A sound at the far end of the room caused him to turn, and he saw his housekeeper enter via the double doors flanked by high bookshelves. Mrs. Rooney looked, as always, peppery and alert, but her gray hair was just a trifle disheveled in contrast to her newly starched apron. The late return last night had interrupted her beauty sleep, she had told them a little tartly.

"Good morning," Rush told her.

"Morning to you, sir. Will you have breakfast?"

"Just coffee for me, Mrs. Rooney. But would you mind going to the guest room and awakening Mrs. Clarken, please? She might want something more than that."

"I saw her in the hall just now, sir. She said coffee was all she wanted."

"Fine. Her husband is on the way over. Make plenty of coffee."

Using the small elevator, he went to his bedroom-study and dressed quickly. He ran the shaver over his face, noticing with scant satisfaction that the lump on the side of his skull had diminished in size. The telephone rang again. Mrs. Rooney had already answered downstairs when Rush picked up the extension. It was Les Montgomery.

"Didn't know if you'd be up, bubba," Montgomery said with nauseating cheerfulness.

"Did you locate him?" Rush asked.

"My ex-cop friend went by the address in Queens. Kind of a crummy place. Nobody there."

"When was that?"

"An hour ago, about."

"He gets going early."

"Well, the rate we're paying the mother—"

"I meant Joe Graeber."

"Oh. Yeah."

"Or maybe he hadn't been back yet from Ohio?"

"Nope, he'd been back. My friend asked around the building. The guy had slept there, or at least he'd been there part of the night, collected a couple of bills out of the mailbox, like that. Then I dunno when he took off again."

"Has he moved?"

"Nope. His stuff is still in there."

"Did your friend go in?"

"Looked through a window. You want him to go in if he can?"

161

"Not at this point. Can he stake it out?"

"Hubba hubba."

"Les, does that, in this case, mean yes?"

"Hubba hubba!"

"Christ. All right."

"Does that mean you want my friend to stake it out?"

"Hubba hubba," Rush replied sarcastically.

"Great!" Montgomery chortled. "Listen. How's everything there?"

"Ask me in an hour or two," Rush said, and hung up.

Going back downstairs, he felt himself bracing inside for what was to come. His watch showed almost 7:30. By driving like a maniac, Dave Clarken would be here very soon. Rush wondered if Dave had even begun to guess at the kind of potential disaster he was hurrying into. For what seemed the millionth time, Rush's mind cycled back over the events, trying to find some solid ray of hope. For the millionth time he found nothing.

In the living room, Jane Clarken stood near the fireplace wall with a cup of black coffee in her hands. She looked very small under the high cathedral ceiling. She wore no makeup; her hair was pulled back simply and severely, with a small gold clip, and her simple pink sundress looked slightly worn and familiar.

She turned to him with startled eyes as he entered, but said nothing. The coffee server was on the table. Rush poured himself a cup.

"I've left those things in the room upstairs," Jane said huskily. "Everything is packed. I brought my own bag down so I can . . . if I leave here now."

The implication was clear enough. "Mrs. Rooney told you Dave is on the way?"

"Yes."

"What do you want done with the things you left upstairs?"

"I don't care. I don't want to see them again."

Rush shrugged. He remembered a time, once, when something very bad had happened. He had driven wildly across the District to reach this house, new then, to pull his clothes off and shower. He remembered scrubbing himself repeatedly, as if getting himself very clean could eliminate the thing that had taken place. Jane was trying to eliminate something with the clothes and suitcases that had accompanied her to Kenton's Run. But the shower had not really worked, had been only mindless ritual. Jane's attempt would not work either.

Jane put down her coffee cup. "He'll be here any minute." She walked around, terribly on edge.

"I want you to remember what I've said," Rush told her.

"I remember, Milo. You're a good friend. But you won't have to lie for me, or withhold anything."

"What are you going to tell him?"

"All of it."

"You might want to tell part, and then later—"

"No." She shook her head vehemently. "There have been enough lies. I won't lie now."

Rush studied her, thinking how incredibly beautiful she was. "He's quite a guy, babe. He can take it."

"You don't know that. Neither do I. Even he couldn't predict what he's going to feel when he knows."

It was true, and the anguish in her eyes was evidence enough. Rush faced her, trying to think of something good and wise to say. There just wasn't anything. He sat down facing the fireplace. She walked to one of the tall bookcases and stared, sightless, at titles.

The chimes sounded distantly. She stiffened.

"Mrs. Rooney will get it," Rush said.

She walked to the center of the room and faced the doors. With visible effort, she squared her shoulders, waiting.

Dave Clarken, wearing shirt and pants that looked as if they had been pulled damp from a dryer, rushed into the room. He glanced toward Milo and then spotted Jane and went to her. "Honey! Are you *all right?*" He reached out and took her hands for a moment, studying her face with intense concern. Then he murmured something and put his arms around her, pulling her close in a protective embrace.

Rush started for the doors to the patio.

Clarken broke the embrace. "Milo! Wait!" He frowned at Jane, then at Rush. "Listen, Milo. Sit down. The three of us have to talk."

"I'm going outside awhile and let you and Jane talk," Rush said, trying to avoid seeing the look on Jane's face. "If you need me, I'll be right out here. Just give me a holler." He was amazed at how casual he sounded.

Clarken looked puzzled. He turned back to his wife. "Honey?"

Her voice faltered. "There's coffee, darling."

Rush opened the sliding door and stepped out onto the shaded patio. Behind him, he heard Clarken speak again, husky with concern.

"Are you all right, baby? What *happened?* Where have you *been?*"

Rush silently closed the door to the room.

There was no good way to tell Clarken any of it, he thought. The shock was going to be intense. It would be a series of shocks, each worse than the last. Some people bore shocks well. Dave Clarken would not fall apart. But Jane had been right: no one could predict.

Rush walked over to the fish pond, a rock-lined pool about ten feet wide and three times as long, with irregular banks shaggy from overhanging ferns. Out of the greeny depths, between lush waterlily pads, the big koi flashed eagerly, popping their broad snouts up in search of feeding. The water frothed red and white, blue, gray, yellow-silver, bronze, crimson, green.

Rush got the sack of trout chow pellets from the table under the eave and sat on a rock, dropping in a handful of pellets at a time. The koi hit them like trout rising for a fly, taking them deep again.

Minutes went by. Rush did not so much as turn to look toward the house. He finished feeding the koi, closed the sack and left it on the rocks beside him, and smoked two cigarettes while he looked out over the garden. The roses were very good. Helen's roses. The thought surprised him, and for an instant it was as if he could see her standing there, tending the roses, the sun like fire in her hair. It was such an unbidden instant of memory that he was shaken by it. In that way she was not dead and would never be dead.

He realized that her memory had sprung so vividly because this was a time when he needed her. She would have been so good with Dave and Jane. She had always known what to say.

Hastily he lighted another cigarette.

More time passed.

"Milo?"

It was Dave Clarken in the patio door. His face looked like white rubber.

Rush walked over and went inside, closing the door behind him. He was drenched from the humid heat of the garden, and the room felt icy.

Dave Clarken stood near the fireplace, his expression dazed from shock. He did not look at Jane, who still sat on the couch. She had been crying.

"We're going home now," Clarken said in an oddly flat tone.

"Fine," Rush said.

Clarken seemed to have trouble getting the words to come out. "I want to . . . thank you. We'll talk . . . later."

Rush didn't say anything.

"Are you ready, Jane?"

She stood and waited.

Clarken looked around as if dazed, then started for the front doors. "Do you have some . . . things?"

"My small bag. In the hall out there."

Clarken held the door for her very formally, stiffly. Rush followed them into the foyer. Clarken picked up the bag. "Thank you," he said again.

"I'll get the door," Rush said.

Jane looked up at him. "Milo—" But whatever she had wanted to say would not come out.

Clarken went out ahead of her, carrying the small suitcase. Rush stood on the porch and watched him put the bag in the back seat of his Volvo, then hold her door for her with the same curious formality. *He was going through motions and she might as well have not been there.*

He walked to his side of the car, got in, closed the door, started the engine. The Volvo pulled away, circling the drive and heading for the tree-lined exit.

Shock, Rush decided. Dave had come to get his wife and take her home, and now he was doing that, automatically, as he had planned. The things she had told him had not had any lasting effect as yet. More lasting effects would come later.

The car vanished down the long, curving driveway, through the trees.

Rush stood on the front porch for a while after it was gone, and then finally went back inside. Dave's lack of reaction, in terms of overt acts, puzzled and worried him. It might have been better if he had shouted or slapped her or stormed out alone. This kind of numbed inaction showed the deepest hurt of all.

Shaking his head, Rush decided the best thing for him to do was try to get it out of his mind for a while. There would be sufficient need for action on his part when Joe Graeber was located. Rush thought he knew how to handle a man of Graeber's caliber to ensure that Jane would not ever be bothered again. That was all he could hope to do. Jane and Dave had to work out their troubled relationship—or find courage to terminate it—on their own.

Checking over sheafs of notes left at the house by Marty, he made several telephone calls on business matters. There had been a serious setback in the Bishop case, and postponements had complicated some others. There were also tapes of a number of telephone calls that he had to play back and make decisions on. He was in his office, just getting ready to start on this line of business, when the intercom buzzed at him.

"Yes, Mrs. Rooney?"

"Sir, Mr. Clarken is here again."

Dave looked as he had before when Milo Rush found him in the living room, except that his expression was more sullen and tortured. There was no handshake. Dave was working hard at controlling things within himself.

"What's on your mind, Dave?"

"It occurred to me, Milo, that maybe I didn't really say thanks. I do thank you for what you did for . . . us."

Rush was more puzzled. "You paid a fee, Dave. It was strictly a job of work."

"I know how much the ordinary client pays for a job like that, if and when he manages to get you to take one on. So I do want to thank you."

"Thanks accepted. What else is on your mind?"

"Nothing. I . . . guess you ought to know, though. I don't

think I'll be over there at the house anymore . . . right now."

"I know it's a hell of a thing to have to try to accept, Dave."

"I just can't face her right now. I don't know if I want to hit her or leave her or *what*. I sat around there, and she sat around there, and we didn't talk or anything else. I was going crazy. I've got to try to work this out. I don't know how."

"Is she all right?"

"I don't know," Dave said, the bitterness showing. "I don't suppose he hurt her any when he stuck it in her."

"Dave."

"I know, I know. Goddamn it, you're supposed to be more mature about things than that, right? Well, I'm not. I look at her and *want* to say it's all right, that we can work it out, but all I see is her in those pictures with those sons of bitches, and then her with that guy in Ohio, and—"

"You understand how she was blackmailed?"

"Yes, but does that make any difference in how I *feel?*"

Rush looked at him. "I guess not."

Dave Clarken sniffed and looked at the floor. "If anything happens, I'll be at the Madison Residence Club. You know the one?"

"Why there?"

"Why not?"

"Stay here," Rush suggested on impulse. "God knows I've got plenty of room."

"I couldn't do that, Milo."

Suddenly it seemed a very good idea. Dave was going to need a friend. They both were. "Why the hell not? I've got rooms upstairs I haven't even been *in* for a year. I'll get Mrs. Rooney to fix you up in one. Don't worry. I'm not going to lecture you."

"I didn't mean that," Clarken said. It was clear by his expression that the idea appealed to him. "But you've done so much already—"

"Do it," Rush said. "Period. Have you got some clothes out in the car?"

"Yes, but—"

" 'But' my ass. Bring them in. You can stay as long as you need to. What you ought to do right now is find a swimsuit in the back bathroom that will fit you, and go take a flying leap into the pool. Swim some laps. Have a drink. Try to unwind a little. You've got it coming."

"I can't relax right now."

"I didn't say you *could*. I said you should *try*. Do you want to come clear out of your tree?"

Despite himself, Clarken smiled nervously. "You make it sound good."

"Then it's settled. I'll tell Mrs. Rooney. We'll have a sandwich or something after a while, if you want one. In the meantime, I'm going to get upstairs for a little while and check some call-master tapes. Use the pool or the bar or whatever. I'll hunt you up when it's lunchtime. Agreed?"

"Milo, God. You're a real friend, and I—"

"What utter shit," Rush grunted, and headed out of the room.

He thought it was a fairly good performance. Just casual enough, just firm enough. Clarken was in bad shape and needed all the help he could get. Just having someone around would be a little help in itself.

Returning to his office, however, Rush conceded to himself that Jane had no such guarantee. She would be over there alone. He could imagine her state of mind. He wished there was something he could do.

Once behind the desk, he started on the tapes again. He dutifully made notes of the first one, then found that he had lost the track on the second and had to play it over. He lost the thread once more. He was thinking about both of them. Mostly, right now, he was wondering what might be going through Jane's mind.

He tried a third time to play the tape, gave up in disgust, and reached for the telephone. It would not hurt for her to know where Dave was. It wouldn't hurt, either, for her to hear a friendly voice. And he wanted to reassure himself that she was in control.

He dialed the number. The telephone rang four times, five, six.

Frowning, he let it ring on.

On the tenth ring she answered. Her voice was husky. "Hello?"

"Hello yourself," Rush said. "I just wanted to see—"

"Hello, Mr. Johnson," she said in the same oddly strained tone. "Thank you for calling, but we really don't need anything this week."

Startled, Rush listened to the silence on the line, trying to figure out what she was talking about.

"Thank you for calling," she said. "Good-bye."

The connection broke.

Rush put down the phone. His first thought was that she had gotten drunk. Unlikely. Her voice had been clear—unmistakably Jane Clarken and unquestionably sober. Could she have not recognized his voice? Hell, no.

He started to punch buttons to call her again. His mind flicked over other possibilities . . . explanations for the way she had sounded and what she had said. 'Johnson'? He didn't know any Johnson. It made no sense. There was no accounting for it, except the faint possibility. . . .

He hung up the telephone and sat there just a second, chilling.

Then he punched the intercom.

"Yes, sir?"

"Find Dave Clarken. Tell him to meet me in the garage. Right now. I mean *right now*, I don't care if he's in the pool or buck naked. I'll explain later."

The gun was still in the suitcase. He punched in fresh slugs, shoved it into his pocket, and went down the back stairs three at a time.

Fourteen

MILO RUSH drove like a maniac.

"Did you call the police?" Dave Clarken demanded, wild-eyed.

"No." Rush skidded the Olds through an intersection.

"You've got a phone in here. Call them."

"And have them go in there with flashing red lights?"

"Couldn't you explain it to them?"

"Maybe I could and maybe I couldn't. Cops are cops. They're great, but they do enjoy going in there with both barrels blasting, and that's exactly what we *can't* afford if my guess is right."

"What do you think—"

"Let me use this phone first, all right?"

"I thought you weren't going to call the police."

"I'm not," Rush said. He slowed down the car long enough to dial.

The call went through swiftly and he got Les Montgomery on the line.

"What's going on?" Montgomery asked.

"Everything. Listen. Is your friend still outside Graeber's flat?"

"Imagine he is, bubba. That's what I told him—"

"Fine. Get to him fast. I mean right now. I want him to go in."

"What do you want out of there?"

"Prints and negatives. You know whose."

"Hubba hubba!"

"Les, I don't know where they might be. Get them. Fast. I don't care what has to be done, or how much of a mess you leave. I want to be absolutely sure you get everything relating to . . . our lady friend."

"I gotcha, boss. My buddy is good at this kind of stuff, and I'll get right out there to make sure myself. Not to worry!"

"I don't know how long you might have, Les."

"Don't sweat it. It's good as done!" The connection broke.

Rush replaced the instrument under the panel and glanced at Clarken. "I don't know what we might find up here. At least we'll have everything he used for blackmailing her. Les and the man he hired will turn that flat inside out."

"Do you think Graeber might . . . hurt her?"

"He might do anything."

"Then go faster, for Christ sake!"

"I'm doing sixty. Will you shut up so I can drive?"

People said you never saw a police officer when you wanted one. Rush did not know right now if he wanted one or not, so he eliminated the possibility from his mind. He drove flat out, taking crazy chances. If a cop tried to flag him for speeding, he thought vaguely, he would have to explain and that would take time. Maybe no one would try to flag him down.

No one did, despite some shocked motorists who had to swerve to get out of his way. He used a series of residential streets, running a dozen or more stop signs, and gunned up the broad thoroughfare that led to the intersection where Dave's street came through.

"I'm going to park two houses down," Rush told Clarken as he slid around the corner. "Can you get around to the back?"

"The Connors have a stockade fence, but I can scale it."

"All right. I'm going up to the front door and I'm going in, right now, no questions asked. Maybe I can take him. Either way, you're our protection. You've got to come in the back without being seen."

Clarken, his face etched with worry, had his hand on the door handle as the car slowed. "I've got it."

Rush hit the brakes and pulled to the curb, remembering to get the key from the ignition. He could see the Clarken house through the overhanging limbs of a huge willow. There was no car in the driveway and everything looked quiet. There was a battered red Pontiac parked across the street.

Clarken got out and started up through the neighbor's yard.

Rush went the other way, along the sidewalk, stifling the impulse to run. That would only draw attention. He had his hand in his pocket on the butt of the gun. He walked up the driveway. He couldn't see any sign of someone watching from the windows. It was very still.

It crossed his mind that they might be much too late. He had to be ready for whatever he might find inside. His teeth gritted together as he thought of possibilities.

He went onto the porch and pulled open the screen. It swung back silently. With a little mental imprecation, he tried the door handle. It did not budge. He got out the gun and slammed it against one of the small panes of glass in the door. The sound was very loud. He reached inside, twisted the handle, and burst into the entry hall.

A chair was overturned in the living room, a drink of something soaking into the couch. The hall toward the rear of the house yawned empty, but as he took the first step in that direction, Joe Graeber appeared in one of the bedroom doorways. He had a revolver in his hand.

Rush swung his own weapon up and snapped the trigger. The gun made a sickening scratchy sound and did not fire. *The mud from the field.*

"Put it down," Graeber ordered. "I mean *right now!*" His hand tightened on the revolver.

Rush dropped his gun to the tiled floor.

"Hands behind your head, move it back here, move slow."

Rush obeyed. Graeber, wearing dark pants and a white dress shirt practically identical to what he had worn during the burglary attempt, was red-faced, his eyes slitted with excitement. He stood back out of reach and gestured with the gun for Rush to move into the bedroom. Rush obeyed again. Graeber followed him in.

The room was astonishingly intact. Patio doors, veiled by light curtains fully drawn against the afternoon sunlight, made everything golden. The room was not large.

Standing beside the bed, eyes wide with horror, was Jane Clarken. She appeared unharmed.

"Milo!" she gasped.

"I thought that's who you were," Graeber said, eyes darting from one of them to the other and back again.

"What are you doing here?" Rush asked.

"I came to even up a score. Now it looks like I get to even up two."

"Against her?" Rush asked, playing for time. "Why not just call the police and give them your old pictures if you want to get back at her?"

"With what she knows now about Ohio? Maybe that's what she was counting on."

"You can't blackmail her anymore now, is that it?"

"You talk a lot. Turn around. Against the wall."

"Milo, don't do it! He'll kill you! He's crazy!"

"Shut up!" Graeber *looked* crazy.

"He's been here almost an hour," Jane said. "Dave is gone and *he* came in, and he's been talking all that time—obscenities—"

Graeber's lips quirked. "Just telling you some of the stuff you got coming to you before I finish with you, you little whore. *I* know you always thought you were better than anybody else. *I* know you pretended to take this job with me, telling this bastard all about it. *I* know how you laughed at me, screwing the whole thing up for me. You think you're so damned—"

The patio doors exploded. Glass flew everywhere. The curtains billowed out and came down, tearing the rods from the wall in a shower of plaster dust, and Dave Clarken came right through them, sprawling forward on the floor. He had an incongruous weapon in his hands: a 2-iron.

Graeber turned, staggered by the flying glass and by the burst of hot outside air, and swung the gun toward Clarken. He might have made it, but Rush had started forward with his first glimpse of moving shadows behind the curtains. His shoulder hit Graeber in the middle, doubling him up and driving him back against the wall. They hit together, hard, and went down. Graeber's gun went off with a deafening crash right in Rush's ear. Stunned by it, Rush nevertheless rolled over and managed to hit Graeber in the side of the head. The big man grunted and brought the gun around.

The 2-iron whistled through a short arc and smashed into the side of Graeber's face. Flesh burst redly. Graeber went down with a thud.

Milo Rush rolled over and got to his feet just in time to see what Clarken was about to do. Rush reached out and caught the golf club in the middle of another swing.

"Let me go!" Clarken rasped. "I'll knock the—"

"*Quit*, Dave! That's enough! He's out cold!"

"I want to hit him again."

"You've done enough. Look at him!"

Clarken bent over and stared. His expression changed magically from excited rage to shock. "God! I've—"

"No, you haven't. But you've done quite enough."

Clarken stared at the bloody iron in his hands. He put it against the wall very gently. "I sneaked up. I stood out there a minute. I heard some of what he said." He turned toward his wife, who stood where she had seemed rooted. "What did he do to you?"

Her hands fluttered in a meaningless gesture. "He thought he had all the time in the world. . . . He just talked . . . crazy."

"Dave," Rush said, "you'd better call the police."

Clarken nodded and went out of the room in a daze.

Jane began to cry without sound, standing there in the same place.

"It's okay now," Rush said.

She nodded and went right on crying.

Rush examined Graeber. The golf club had done massive damage to his jaw, but his breathing was all right and there was no sign, superficially at least, of brain damage. Unconscious, the man had a serene and untroubled look. Rush found the gun on the floor and carried it into the other room, using his handkerchief. His own revolver was still on the tile floor. He decided it might be better to leave it there. The police were picky about the scene.

Jane came out of the bedroom and sat limply on the couch. In the kitchen Dave's voice could be heard, low and jerky with tension. In a minute he came back into the living room. He ran his hand nervously through his hair.

"I told them we had an intruder. I didn't say much more. I didn't know what to tell them."

Rush thought about it a moment. "He worked where Jane worked a long time ago. There was an old grudge because she wouldn't go out with him. He had been drinking. That's all true."

"That's not all of it."

"It ought to be enough."

"He'll tell them about the—the other things."

"I don't think so. He can't say anything without incriminating himself, and he isn't going to get out of this one. Judges take a dim view of first-degree burglary these days, and with the gun a charge of attempted armed robbery might stick, too."

Clarken looked at his wife, then back at Rush. "I tried to find a weapon. My golf clubs were back there in the storage shed. I couldn't find anything better. I felt like a damned fool. Then I came through the glass—" He stopped and looked down at his hands, palms up. They were bleeding profusely.

"Dave!" Jane cried. "I'll get something." She hurried toward the bathroom.

Clarken sat down. "I think maybe I'm going to get sick."

"Try not to," Rush said mildly, "but if you have to, hold it off at least until I've gotten out of the room."

"Where are you going?"

"Telephone call."

Clarken hung his head.

The telephone in the kitchen was a wall instrument, push buttons. Rush tapped out his office number. Marty answered promptly.

"Have you heard from Les?" Rush asked.

"He just called this instant."

"What did he say?"

"He said to tell you, if you called, all the eggs were in one basket and he has the basket safe and sound." Marty sounded puzzled.

Rush grinned. "Thanks, babe. He does work fast, doesn't he?"

"I don't know what he *meant*," Marty replied indignantly.

"What if I explain over dinner?"

"I guess I should play hard to get. I accept."

Rush walked back into the living room. He intended to tell them immediately that Les had found the pictures and negatives—that they were in safe hands and the threat of blackmail from that direction had been eliminated. But he saw that he had walked into something else. He paused by the door and said nothing.

Jane had returned with towels and a basin and was kneeling in front of Dave, wiping away the blood with infinite care. Dave was watching her face, showing no sign of what had to be pain.

"Hey," he said softly.

She looked up at him.

"I was nuts," he told her.

She didn't say anything, but her eyes desperately searched his face.

He said, "We're going to work this out. We are, right? I mean, we're just going to work this whole goddamned thing *out*."

"Yes," she whispered.

They looked at each other almost stubbornly. They knew it was not going to be easy. But they meant it.

Milo Rush took a deep breath and felt himself relaxing. In the distance the police siren wailed.